Heirs of Catriona

Heirs of Catriona

Anusha Subramanian

Celebrating
30 Years of Publishing
in India

First published in 2012

This edition published in India by HarperCollins *Publishers* in 2023
4th Floor, Tower A, Building No. 10, Phase II, DLF Cyber City,
Gurugram, Haryana – 122002
www.harpercollins.co.in

2 4 6 8 10 9 7 5 3 1

Copyright © Ravi Subramanian 2012, 2016, 2023

P-ISBN: 978-93-5629-470-7
E-ISBN: 978-93-5629-471-4

This is a work of fiction and all characters and incidents described in this book are the product of the author's imagination. Any resemblance to actual persons, living or dead, is entirely coincidental.

Anusha Subramanian asserts the moral right
to be identified as the author of this work.

All rights reserved. No part of this publication may be reproduced, stored in a retrieval system, or transmitted, in any form or by any means, electronic, mechanical, photocopying, recording or otherwise, without the prior permission of the publishers.

Printed and bound at
Manipal Technologies Limited, Manipal

This book is produced from independently certified FSC® paper to ensure responsible forest management.

To Meghna and Manya, my younger sisters, who will one day grow up and read this book.
And
To my amazing family and wonderful friends for their constant support, encouragement and enthusiasm.

1

The sun streamed in through the windows of the small one-bedroom apartment. It was a beautiful morning—the birds chirped and the flowers did their bit by letting loose a sweet fragrance. Sara loved waking up like this. She sat up in bed and shook open her long beautiful brown hair. As was her habit, her fingers reached for the intricately carved necklace with a butterfly pendant that hung around her neck. The pendant was a unique shade of cerulean blue. It had tiny holes in it, but the stones to be embedded in them were missing. Sara's mother had given it to her when she was just a little girl. Now she was eighteen; a strikingly beautiful teenager with coffee brown eyes and dark hair that cascaded down to her slim waist.

Sara turned to where her golden retriever pup, Jasmine, lay fast asleep. True to her name, like a blooming jasmine flower, she was spotlessly white. She scooped Jasmine up in her arms and patted her shiny little head. Then she put her down and pulled open a small chest of drawers beside her bed. Inside, lying on a cane mat, was a, dog-eared, pale pink diary. On the diary, a name was penned in flowing script: *ANASTASIA*. It had once belonged to her mother. There was a dry leaf sticking out of one of the pages. Sara picked up the diary and opened it to the page marked by the leaf. The page had a tiny rose imprint on one corner, and underneath that, an inscription:

Beyond the magical picture
There is a world
To enter which
People for centuries
Have tried to figure.
Beyond waterfalls and lakes
There lies a castle
To fathom its treasures
Is beyond mind's measure.

Then there was a message, which seemed to have been scribbled in a hurry:

I gave you everything you asked for and left you with something priceless. I had to hide it in a special place as the law forbids me to tell you about it until you come of age. But I don't think I will be here till then...

Sara read these words every day. At least thrice a day, she picked up the diary and looked at the message. But she never understood any of it.

She still remembered the day she lost her mom. She was only eight. It was the day she, along with her classmates, was singing for a school talent show. They had bagged the Best

Talent award and the team was ecstatic. They had celebrated at the school canteen and afterwards, she had run home to tell her mother. But when she arrived, the house was empty. There was no mom waiting for her. She ran to her best friend Crystal's house. Their mothers were fast friends and usually went everywhere together. But Crystal's mom was out too. In vain the two girls waited, and searched everywhere.

Their mothers never returned home. The search extended well into the night, then into the next day, and the next, and the next, till the girls were convinced there was no way their mums were ever returning alive.

Sara felt a drop of tear on her cheek as she remembered the last of the happy moments she had spent with her mom.

Just then a voice shook her out of her trance.

'Sara…hey, Sara?'

2

'Crystal!' cried Sara. Jasmine jumped up to meet Crystal, overjoyed, and ran around her in circles, barking her approval.

Crystal was her best friend, no, they were more than that. They were soul sisters. Crystal too had a similar necklace like Sara's, given to her by her mother. Crystal had glossy, jet black hair, warm dark-brown eyes and the body of an athlete, slim and long. Their mothers had been related and they were practically cousins. But they were never told exactly how they were related. It was far too complex and intricate a relationship to comprehend. Their moms would spend hours together and so would the children

And now years after their moms had left them they were still together. They went to the same college and worked together at the same job. Crystal was Sara's partner in the small odd jobs business that they had set up together in Sara's backyard. They ran errands for people for a small fee. The business was doing fairly well.

'Ready for college?' asked Crystal.

'Do I look like I am?' answered Sara, grinning.

'Um....not really! Fine then, I'll meet you outside my house in thirty minutes,' Crystal said, running off to get ready.

Sara got dressed hurriedly and in thirty minutes, she was standing outside Crystal's door. In a few minutes, Crystal appeared, dressed in a pair of skinny jeans and a black top. 'Is that a Mango?' she asked Sara.

'Yeah! How'd you guess?' Sara asked.

'Because I'm awesome!' laughed Crystal.

'Yeah, right! Come on now, we are getting late for college,'

'Bye Jasmine,' she called out to her dog who was peeping from the door.

The college where they studied had a huge campus. As the two of them entered, a tall, lean boy came running towards them. He had dark unruly hair, caramel skin, and warm brown eyes that twinkled with mischievous humour.

He stopped in front of them and winked.

Sara and Crystal high-fived him.

'Wassup, Kyran?' Sara said.

'Sup,' Crystal added.

'Nothing much. I walk a lonely road...the only one that I have ever known...' Kyran began, singing a verse from a popular track 'Boulevard of Broken Dreams'.

'Well, your hair's grown,' Crystal interrupted. 'Looks good.'

Sara nodded.

Kyran brightened. 'I know! It looks so cool, doesn't it?' He ruffled his dark hair.

'So, what have you been up to?' Crystal asked, a little suspicious of the mischievous twinkle in Kyran's eyes.

'Nothing. Just—,' At that instant, a piercing scream split the air, drowning out his voice.

'That's the new Geography teacher,' Kyran said, smiling devilishly, as the scream died down. 'She just discovered the Fevicol in her hair.'

'Kyran! You didn't!' Sara gasped.

'What? She was driving me nuts when I met her this morning!' Kyran shrugged. Then he pinched his nose and mimicked the Geography teacher's nasal voice, '*Dear* boy, you must know the capital of the Republic of Zagreb! No? Oh, you are as thick as the castles of Scotland!'

The girls laughed.

Kyran was their closest friend. He lived with his uncle nearby. Although he was constantly praising himself and calling himself handsome, the girls knew that he was not vain. He could be charming when he wanted but he could also make his point firmly and politely if required.

The bell rang.

'See you, guys. I have History now.' Crystal walked away.

'Come on Kyran, we have Culture and Mythology,' Sara turned to go to class, Kyran behind her.

The day dragged slowly on until finally, the last bell rang. As the students filed out of the classes Crystal, Sara and Kyran caught up with one another. They walked back home, laughing and joking about the day gone by.

'See you tomorrow guys!' Kyran shouted as he continued down the road after dropping Sara and Crystal home. As if in a trance, Sara kept looking in the direction in which Kyran was heading. A strange fear had taken over her; a fear which made her feel that it would be a long time before she saw Kyran again.

'Sara? You ok?' Crystal asked, peering at her, concerned.

Sara shook herself. *Just a stupid feeling,* she thought. But she couldn't help thinking about it. Maybe, just maybe, this was a premonition.

Crystal was still staring at her. 'I'm ok. Just tired after college,' she answered casually, still not taking her eyes off the tiny figure of her dearest friend disappearing in the distance.

~

'Meet you in five minutes!' shouted Sara as she and Crystal went into their respective apartments. Within five minutes both of them had changed and were at the shop from where they ran their business. It wasn't very big; at best it could be called a stall. 'Odd Jobs' was written in large letters across a board on top. They also sold homemade lemonade and fruit juices from the stall.

'Hey Venus, how's life?' asked Crystal. Their neighbour, Venus, had just walked into the store carrying a few shirts. Jasmine ran to greet Venus, who was a favourite customer since she always brought treats. She busied herself trying to look for treats in Venus's pockets.

'Good. How are you both?' Venus smiled. 'Just wanted the buttons sewed on these couple of shirts and of course I would like a glass of your lemonade.' She laughed when she saw what Jasmine was doing.

'Jasmine, I hid your treats somewhere else this time!'

Jasmine barked in excitement and her lips peeled back into what looked almost like a smile. Venus laughed again. 'Here, girl, here are your treats!' she put her hand into her purse and took out a handful of dog biscuits and held them out for Jasmine. 'Woof!' barked Jasmine joyously and wolfed down the biscuits.

'Really, Venus! You spoil her! I'll get the lemonade from the house. I forgot to get it today!' Sara grinned as she dashed inside to get the jug of cold lemonade.

When she came back, she noticed Crystal talking to a strangely-dressed old man. Sara poured out a glass of lemonade for Venus and handed it to her.

"Thanks. See you, I'll come later to collect the shirts," Venus said, as she headed out. Sara nodded absently. Then she turned to Crystal and saw that she had a puzzled expression on her face.

'What's wrong?' she asked.

Crystal took her aside. 'You saw that old man I was talking to? He suddenly appeared out of nowhere and said he wants to talk to us. He claims he knows our mothers,' she whispered, looking spooked.

'What? That's weird,' Sara was surprised.

'Young ladies, please hear me out before you decide anything about me.'

The old man had sensed their discomfort and had walked up to them. Jasmine bared her teeth and growled at him. Sara gave her a quick pat. 'It's okay, Jasmine, take it easy for now,' she whispered. 'Why don't you stand guard while Crystal and I sort this out?' Obediently, Jasmine withdrew and stood a few feet away from them, on guard.

The old man was a strange sight. He was dressed like an ancient Roman. He wore a flowing white toga and wooden sandals. He had a bumpy nose and black, watery, bird-like eyes. Altogether, thought Sara, he looked as if he had been transported from another place and time and plonked down in the modern world.

The man sighed. 'Ask me whatever you want about your mothers,' he said. 'I am willing to answer any question that will make you trust me.'

Crystal put one hand on her hips. 'If you can tell us our mothers' first names, we'll trust you,' she said.

The old man smiled. He wagged a finger at Sara. 'Your mom's name is Anastasia, am I right?' Sara nodded. He turned his gaze towards Crystal and continued, 'And young lady, your mother's name is Olivia,' he smiled.

Not too many people had known these names, their mothers were known mostly by their nicknames. So the girls looked at each other in disbelief. This man certainly seemed to know something about their moms.

'One sec,' said Sara and she dashed to the store to pull down its shutters. She was back in an instant and looked at the old man. 'Come in please,' she invited him inside. Then she whistled and Jasmine came to heel, still looking suspiciously at the old stranger.

The three of them went inside Sara's house. She gestured at three chairs around a small glass table, inviting him to sit. Jasmine settled herself on her favourite rug opposite the old man. From there she could keep an eye on him, in case he tried something funny. The man made himself comfortable, but Crystal remained standing.

'Aren't you going to sit?' he asked, smiling.

'No thanks, I'm fine,' Crystal was still defensive. 'About our mothers...'

'Yes, yes! But before that, how about some tea?' The old man sank deeper into the soft leather chair. Crystal's face grew red with anger. *If this was some kind of a lame joke, then Mr Old Man had better watch out because she would personally wring his neck.* But before she could speak, Sara intervened, 'Of course! Why don't you and Crystal chat while I go get some tea?' She poked Crystal in the back.

'Let me go and make the tea!' Crystal hissed. 'If I stay here any longer I swear I'll go nuts!'

Sara smiled 'Come on! You'll be fine!'

'But he's bonkers!' whispered Crystal as Sara walked into the kitchen.

As Sara made tea, Crystal tried her best to make conversation. But it was difficult. The man hardly said a word! The long silence was interspersed by the sounds from the kitchen. It was frustrating.

'So where are you from?' she asked after five minutes of silence, just as Sara came out of the kitchen with three cups of tea.

'Catriona,' said the old man.

'Umm…is that somewhere near—well, I don't know—the North Pole or something? Or Antarctica maybe?' asked Sara, as she finished serving the tea and sat down. Her voice dripped with sarcasm. She was hopeless at Geography, but this was going too far.

'No, no! It's not anywhere in this world!' the old man replied cheerfully as he sipped his tea. 'Excellent tea, I must say!' And he smiled mysteriously.

'I told you…he's nuts!' Crystal muttered to Sara.

'I think I believe you now,' Sara whispered back.

'I heard that!' said the old man, smiling. 'And believe me, I get that a lot!' He laughed as Sara and Crystal blushed, very embarrassed.

'So what do you want to tell us?' Sara asked, trying to change the topic quickly.

The old man smiled. 'I knew your mothers well. Nice young women. I needed to tell you something that they had asked me to tell you.'

His next words made the girls gasp. 'You are no ordinary children. In fact, your families were never ordinary families. Both of you have something mystical and magical inside you.'

Sara and Crystal looked at each other, confused smiles playing on their lips. They had read stories of magic and mystery, of course, but this old man was saying that there was something supernatural about them. Was he out of his mind?

'And girls,' continued the old man, pulling them out of the thoughts they had got lost in, 'Now you need to embark on a journey. You see, Catriona is in grave danger, and needs *you* to save it!' Here he paused and seemed to gather his breath. Then he made a pronouncement that made the girls jump to their feet in surprise:

'Your mothers are not dead!'

'What?' cried Sara. 'Are you insane?'

'No, no, my dear! I certainly am not!' the old man said cheerily. 'But do believe me. Your mothers and the land of Catriona are in great danger. They are imprisoned, forced to do the bidding of the evil witch who has taken over the throne!'

Sara stared at the old man for a few minutes. She noticed that the merry twinkle had gone out of his eyes. She wanted to believe what he was saying with all her heart, but she was afraid of hoping. But if what the old man was saying was true…and if their mothers were in danger…if they were not rescued in time it would be too painful to lose them all over again, because the girls didn't believe in the man's warning.

Crystal looked shocked as well. But before they could say anything more, he handed them a piece of paper. On it was written:

Aquamarine

Zircon

Turquoise

Sapphire

'Huh?' said Sara, squinting at the piece of paper. 'What *is* this?'

The old man smiled once again. There was something strange about his smile. The glitter in his eyes seemed to tell Sara and Crystal that there was some truth in what he was saying. Yet what he had just told them was still hard to believe!

As if he could read their minds, the old man said, 'These are going to help you.' He was pointing at the necklaces that hung from each of their necks.

'Pictures are entrances,' he said. Then he turned to Sara and asked her, 'What did your mom leave for you, Sara?' She was confused. Was he asking her or was he making a statement? Neither of them could tell.

'Pictures are entrances? What are you talking about?' she asked, puzzled.

The old man shook his head. 'My work is done here,' he said abruptly.

The very moment he said those words a strange light radiated from his eyes, so intense that it nearly blinded Sara and Crystal. Almost in unison, they raised their hands and covered their eyes to protect them from the sting of the blinding rays. By the time the light subsided and the two of them could see again, the old man had vanished.

~

'What the...' Crystal began, amazed. 'Magical families, Catriona, mysterious necklaces and now some weird riddle! One moment our moms are supposed to be dead and poof! What do you know? They are not dead after all! What's going on?'

'Woof?' Jasmine cocked her head and barked, looking confused as well. She trotted over to Sara and sat down heavily on her feet.

'I think we should check it out. He did know their names, which not many people know,' Sara tried to reason with Crystal.

'You have to agree, the old man wasn't too clear about anything. What are we supposed to do? How do we save this magical realm of Catriona? Why are we supposed to save it? What have we got to do with it?' Crystal banged her fist emphatically on the wooden table with every question.

'And how do we enter Catriona? We don't even know the way.' Crystal continued without letting Sara get a word in. 'He said that pictures are entrances... Was that a clue?'

'Questions, questions and more questions!' Sara's forehead had wrinkled up. She was thinking very hard.

'What do you think he meant by pictures are entrances?' Crystal asked again. This one had left them both stumped.

'I think it means that the entrance to Catriona is through a picture.' Sara said.

'So, obviously, it's not going to be a simple picture of cute puppies or something, right?'

Sara smiled at Crystal. 'No, I think it ... it has to be connected to Catriona in some way…and if it's connected to Catriona, then that means it has to be connected to our mothers.'

Suddenly Crystal's eyes lit up. 'And if it is connected to our mothers it has to be connected to…'

'Us!' Sara completed the sentence.

'Bingo!' shouted Crystal. 'It has to be connected to us!' she beamed at Sara.

'Connected to us, huh?' Sara thought aloud. 'What could it be?'

'The thing is, it shouldn't be so difficult!'

'How can you be so sure?' Sara asked skeptically.

'Idiot! Just think. If Catriona really *does* exist and they really do need our help then why would they give us a really difficult clue?' Crystal paused, thinking as she was speaking. 'We may never be able to solve it. What do you think they will do then?'

Sara still had a thoughtful look on her face.

'Sara, I don't think these Catrionians are super smart, or why would they need help? But I don't think they are dumb either. They wouldn't risk us not being able to solve the clue. That's why I think the solution to the clue has to be right in front of our eyes.'

'You have a point,' Sara said. 'So let's do this—since he said "pictures are entrances", we'll take out all the pictures that we have and look through them to see if we can figure something out.'

'Good idea,' Crystal said.

'Our *only* idea,' Sara pointed out.

The two girls got down to work. Jasmine lay dozing in a corner, excessively bored by the activity that did not involve her at all.

'Is that all?' asked Sara after half an hour of hectic searching. A pile of portraits, paintings, still life and drawings lay haphazardly in front of her.

'Pretty much,' Crystal replied, eyeing the pile with disgust, and dusting her grimy hands.

'Not much to start with, huh?'

'Yeah, but we can't do anything about that,' said Crystal. 'Let's sort through what we have for now.'

They worked their way through the pile. There were still life paintings and nature drawings, pencil sketches and glass paintings, mostly painted by Sara's mum. There were pictures of Sara and Crystal at various ages but none of their mothers. They sifted through the pictures for hours, trying to make sense of what the old man had said.

'I'm getting something to eat, I am *so* hungry,' Crystal said suddenly and got up. As she rushed to the kitchen, she stepped on an oil painting of the two of them. She slipped on the picture, tried to stop herself from falling and in the process, scraped her toenail against the picture. The nail broke but not without peeling off a chunk of paint from the canvas.

'Ow!' Crystal collapsed on the floor, holding her foot in her right hand.

'Woof! Woof!' Jasmine woke up and barked suddenly. She gave Crystal a look of disgust before settling back down for another doze.

'Are you alright?' Sara asked, concerned.

'Well, if you consider breaking a nail alright, I guess I'm 'superb,' Crystal snapped, examining her nail. She was expecting Sara to show some sympathy and make her feel better, but when she looked up, she saw Sara was not even looking at her. She wasn't even listening any more. Instead, she was staring at the canvas that Crystal had slipped on. She bent down and picked it up. Crystal got up and walked towards Sara wondering what she was up to. She looked over Sara's shoulder. The scratch from Crystal's toenail had cut across the canvas. Underneath, there wasn't the usual white canvas. Instead, it was dark brown. It was a tiny detail, so easy to miss. But Sara had a sharp eye for detail.

Even as Crystal stared, Sara leaned forward. Her heart was thudding with excitement.

Crystal tapped her on the shoulder. 'What's up?' she asked, puzzled.

'I think you would want to take a look at this,' Sara said gravely, and held the painting up against the light. Crystal gasped. Painted behind the picture of Sara and Crystal, shone a shadowy silhouette of two regal women.

'Oh my God,' Sara whispered, awestruck.

'Does this mean that our photo was painted on top of another?' Crystal asked. 'Let's start scraping,' she added.

'Wait.' Sara put the picture down and walked into the kitchen. In a jiffy she was back. In her left hand was a rag cloth and in her right, a pot full of fragrant oil.

'Dude, we've got a job at hand, now is not the time to oil your hair,' Crystal said.

'No, you idiot! You know Mom was a passionate painter. This was her special, or you can say secret, mixture, which she used to correct mistakes or smooth the paint. She told no one about this, except, of course *your* mom. I don't know what to do with it, so I use it for my hair. That's why I have some of it with me.'

'How will it help?' Crystal asked.

'We can use this to remove the image on top of the original painting without damaging what lies underneath.'

Crystal beamed. 'Rub away, sis!'

Sara got down to work. Slowly but steadily she started clearing away the paintdipping the rag into the oil and rubbing it gently on the photo. Ten minutes of careful scrubbing and she was able to fully uncover the secret picture. It was quite astonishing.

It was a portrait of two stunningly beautiful women. The artist had painted them only up to their waists. One of them had a flawless complexion, locks of dark brown hair that fell in layers and matched her coffee-brown eyes. She wore a wine coloured gown decorated with frills and lace. A sparkling diamond necklace adorned her neck. The second woman had a slightly bronzed skin and dark hair. She wore a turquoise coloured gown laced with tiny pearls. A single string of white pearls hung around her neck. Both the ladies held delicate wine glasses in their hands, half filled with red wine, in the act of raising a toast. They looked very happy together.

'I think I know them,' Crystal said slowly, staring at the beautiful picture.

'We know them too well Crystal,' Sara said, her voice grave.

'Mom,' Sara said softly.

'Mom,' Crystal whispered her response. 'Where did the two of you disappear?'

A stunned silence followed. Then Crystal said, 'Yeah, it does look like them. But why are they dressed in these... these costumes? They are dressed like queens!'

Sara smiled. 'Pictures are entrances,' she said with her mouth upturned in a wide grin.

'The old tramp also asked you what your mom left for you, Sara. What was it? Think, Sara. Think!' Crystal pressed on.

'I really don't know of anything that my mom left for me except the note in the diary...'

'*Of course!*' Crystal grinned. 'That's the thing! Get it. *Now!*'

Sara ran and got the note. 'Okay, but what are we supposed to do with these?' Crystal asked.

'First let's hang up this painting and then I guess we read this poem,' said Sara, shrugging.

Before they started reciting the poem in front of the picture, Sara remembered the paper the old man had given them. Hurriedly, she went and got it. Crystal ran to get her backpack in which she had packed water, some chips, a notebook and a pen, their iPods and other odds and ends.

Sara walked over to Jasmine. 'Wake up, darling,' Sara cooed softly in her ear. Jasmine lifted her head from her paws and walked groggily up to Crystal.

'I don't know what is going to happen. It's better to be prepared,' warned Sara.

Standing in front of the painting, they closed their eyes and recited the poem. Nothing happened. Sara glanced at Crystal. She had a worried look on her face. Both of them nodded and said the poem once more. Still nothing. Sara's shoulders sagged, she was losing hope. Crystal lifted her right hand, brought it up to Sara's shoulder, and nodded, meaning, *Let's try this one last time.* They folded their hands and said the poem again for the third time.

∞

3

All of a sudden a soft purple light filled the room. They felt themselves being pulled into empty space. They were in a swirling mist of purple light. Then a rainbow staircase, spiraling downwards, appeared before them.

Jasmine was scared now, and started barking loudly. Sara scooped up the howling Jasmine in her arms. Jasmine kicked and barked hysterically but she held on to her, not letting go.

Slowly they started climbing down the stairs. After a long time, they saw the last step of the staircase up ahead. As soon as Sara and Crystal reached the bottom of the staircase, it disappeared.

'Wow,' said Crystal, amazed.

'Wow is the word.' agreed Sara.

Jasmine had stopped howling. Now, she cocked her head and surveyed the scene in front of her.

They were in a beautiful land—prettier than anything they had ever seen in their lives. Up ahead was a waterfall with crystal clear water cascading down into a small lake. A lush green forest spread around it, as far as the eye could see. They could also see some small huts in the distance. Faint sounds of laughter wafted through their open windows. Sara turned around and with a start, saw the facade of an immense castle rising majestically behind her.

'Wait a minute!' she exclaimed. Her eyes opened wide as she pointed excitedly towards the castle.

'Wow,' exclaimed Crystal. 'It's so pretty.'

'Forget that, you idiot, can't you see?'

'What?'

'Dude, the castle! Don't you remember? The...the...' Sara stammered in excitement.

'Excuse me?' said Crystal. She didn't understand even a bit!

Beyond Waterfalls and lakes
There lies a castle in all its glory
To fathom its many treasures
Is beyond the mind's measure.

Remember?'

'Oh yeah... how could I forget?' It was all coming back to Crystal now.

'Mom was talking about *this* castle! What are we waiting for? Let's get going!'

They began walking towards it. It was further than it looked. At last, about an hour later, they reached the castle gates.

'Now what?' asked Crystal.

'How am I supposed to know? I guess we have to go inside,' said Sara. But as she began walking up to the guard to ask him to let them in, a horrible, screeching voice from the castle made her stop in her tracks.

'You idiot!' screamed the voice, 'Now your head will roll! I asked for a midnight blue dress with moonbeams sewn in and see what you've brought me! This is a shade lighter than midnight blue! And where are the moonbeams? And see, this stitch out of place! How dare you bring something like this to me!'

A trembling voice answered, 'B-b-but y-y-your m-m-majesty...'

'Shut up! How dare you answer me back?' cried the terrible voice again. 'Have his hands dipped in boiling oil. That's the punishment for stitching me a thing like that and then answering back!'

The trembling voice pleaded, 'Pardon me, your majesty! I have my wife and children to feed! Please, your majesty, *please* pardon me!'

'Get out of my sight! You are not getting a pardon. This will set a good example to the people who think they can challenge me!' cried the horrible voice.

Sara strained to hear another feeble voice that probably belonged to one of the guards guarding the palace.

'Poor chap! Everyone knows getting moonbeams and midnight blue cloth is impossible. The sky fairies won't let *anyone* near their house.'

'I'm not sure I want to go in,' whispered Sara to Crystal. Jasmine whimpered in agreement.

It was too late.

'Hey, you girls!' called out a palace guard.

'Uh-oh... *Run*! Now!' The two girls and Jasmine turned

around and started running.

They ran fast with Sara in the lead and Crystal and Jasmine close behind. Sara turned back to see if the guards were left behind. She saw Crystal stretching out her hand as if she was trying to tell her something. And before she knew it, Sara had tripped on a rock that was jutting six inches out of the ground. Crystal collided into her and both of them fell headfirst and blacked out.

'Woof! Woof!' Jasmine ran up to them, confused.

'Idiot! I was trying to tell you to watch...yourr ...sstepp,' Crystal drawled before blacking out.

4

Sara woke up to see two faces peering at her. One was a man's and the other was a beautiful girl's.

'Aaaahhhh!!' screamed Sara.

'Keep quiet, girl!' said the man, sternly.

'Who are you?' Sara asked, gathering up her courage.

The man was tall and muscular. The girl looked at Sara kindly through long, black lashes. She was the prettiest girl Sara had ever seen. 'I am Rose and he is Peter,' said the girl, extending her hand.

'Really nice to meet you,' said Sara shaking her hand, wondering why she was there and who they were.

'Jasmine!' said Sara suddenly, 'Where's Jasmine?'

'One moment please,' said Peter and went into the kitchen. He returned carrying a tiny jasmine flower.

'For you,' he said, bowing.

Sara took the flower.

'Umm....uh.....thanks...but this isn't exactly what I'm

looking for,' she said, sheepishly. 'I was actually looking for my dog.'

'But you said jasmine,' Peter looked a bit abashed.

'Well yes, because it's my dog's name.'

'Oh we found him beside you, licking your face,' Rose said. 'He's in the kitchen eating some fruits,' added Peter.

'*She* is in the kitchen you mean. Jasmine? Eating *fruits*? Wow!'

Peter who had disappeared into the kitchen returned with a white bundle of fur in his arms. As soon as Jasmine saw Sara she leapt right into her lap with a happy bark and gave her a huge, wet lick.

'Um...' said a familiar voice, 'I hope I'm not intruding but may I know who both of you are?' It was Crystal, who spoke with mock politeness. She had just woken up and was startled to see the two strangers. Rose and Peter introduced themselves again. Jasmine bounded from Sara's lap to Crystal's, overjoyed to see her friends awake at last.

'This is our house. You are safe now. We rescued you from the soldiers,' said Peter.

Seeing the blank look on their faces, he continued, 'Both of you blacked out as soon as you hit the ground. The guards found you and would have captured you and taken you to the place to be presented before the queen. And that, believe me, would *not* have been good. But luckily we intervened.'

'Yes, we reached you just before the guards and managed to pull you into some bushes to hide you from them. They take their jobs pretty seriously,' Rose said, looking grave.

'But wait! Who was the one screaming in the palace? And is the queen all that bad? Why is she the queen then?' asked Crystal.

Suddenly Sara remembered what that old man had said about the 'wicked witch' who had taken over the throne.

'It's that witch, isn't it?' she asked, 'who has taken over the throne? What happened to the real queen and how are our mothers connected with all this?'

Rose sighed. 'Any more questions?'

'Oh, and why were the guards chasing us?' Sara asked, crossing her arms.

'The "wicked witch", who is now our queen, is Merissa. She was the one you heard screaming in the palace. And as to whether the queen is "all that bad", well...you should have got the answer when you overheard her screaming,' Peter answered.

Sara and Crystal shuddered visibly as they remembered the hideous punishment the queen had pronounced on the poor tailor who had stitched that gown.

'According to the new law, anyone who comes within a mile of the palace without a permit, are to be handcuffed and brought before the queen. That's why the guards were chasing you. And you did nothing to allay the suspicion of the guards by running like that! But I don't blame you. After hearing the queen scream like that, anyone would...You certainly did better to run than to get captured,' Rose said. 'A lot has changed here since the queen seized control.'

Peter shook his head sadly. 'Catriona is certainly not the same without Anastasia and Olivia.'

'What? You knew our mothers!' Sara could barely conceal her surprise.

'Finally! Some news about our mothers! Now will you please tell us where they are and how are they connected with Catriona?' Crystal demanded.

But Sara still shook her head, confused. 'What *is* going on here? How will we find our mothers? Where are they? Why were we called here and what are we supposed to do?'

'I can try to answer some of the questions,' said Peter. Then he began, 'Here in Catriona...'

'It's a nice place, Catriona' interrupted Sara.

'Yes, thank you. Now, will you please let me continue?' Peter asked, a little impatiently.

'Sorry.'

Peter continued:

'Once upon a time Catriona was ruled by two good sisters. But their childhood friend Merissa was forever plotting to overthrow them and rule in their place. Finally one day she managed to do so.'

'Uh...how did she manage to do that? Please elaborate,' Crystal interrupted.

'Oh, the usual!' said Rose, waving a hand impatiently. 'By using dark magic and forbidden enchantments and treachery.'

Peter inclined his head slightly and asked if he may continue. Crystal nodded.

'There were rumours that Merissa had killed the sisters but there were quite a few people who believed that they were alive and had been imprisoned by the queen. The Catrionians—people of Catriona—didn't want to believe that the two queens were dead. They were very dear to their subjects, you see, and most Catrionians hated Merissa with a vengeance. You, Sara and Crystal, are the daughters of these two queens.'

A strangled gasp rose from Sara and Crystal's face began to grow steadily paler.

'Now, Catriona, ruled by Merissa, was in grave danger,

overrun by evil beings unleashed by the new queen's dark magic,' Peter continued, oblivious to their reactions. 'The forests were dying; the sea creatures were being poisoned; even the wind was refusing to blow. And as Catriona fell to ruin, Merissa and her court shut themselves away in the lavish palace, throwing extravagant parties and living a life of pleasure.'

But Crystal hardly heard the rest of his story. 'We are...princesses,' she said, dazed.

Peter looked at the two of them thoughtfully and said, 'We have been waiting long for you to come and make things the way they were. The prophecy said so.'

'What prophecy? And how do you know about it?'

'This prophecy was made hundreds of years ago. But no one heeded it then. Rose and I work at the palace; I as a gardener and Rose as a cook. Before Merissa's rule, we were the queens' most trusted advisors. We were their confidantes. They had probably sensed Merissa's evil intentions, I honestly don't know if they did, but in the last days of their rule, they told us that their daughters would come. And when they did, we were supposed to tell them enough to help them on their quest to save Catriona and its people. They told us to tell you that if you ever have to make a choice between your mothers and the people of Catriona, choose the people.'

'Wait a sec!' Sara cut in, her face anxious. 'This is all a huge mistake. Our mothers were not queens!'

But even as she said this, she knew that Peter was telling the truth. Small things came back to her now...The way her mother always carried herself regally, how being ordered about or even the slightest hint of an accusation would bring out the defiance that was so prominent in her personality. All these had been bred into her—the true traits of a queen.

'Now understand this,' Peter continued. 'Merissa didn't become queen just like that. It would have taken a very powerful magician to defeat your mothers and Merissa isn't a very powerful magician on her own. At least she can't do *good* magic well. She had always been up to her neck in the dark arts. When she seized the throne, she cast such a powerful spell that nothing in the world could defeat her. It was a spell so dark, that nothing could defeat her. The evil queen that she was, she cast this spell tapping into the energy reserves of her supporters' bodies. There were fifteen of them, six of them lost their lives and one was so traumatized that he turned mad.'

'If she cannot be defeated, does that mean we cannot free our mothers? Why are we here then?'

'Melissa overlooked one little thing. Something, which when created, is powerful enough to defeat her. The "Moon Wand".'

'The Moon Wand?' Sara and Crystal chorused.

'Yes. You can defeat Merissa only if you create the magical Moon Wand. Your necklaces and this book will help you.'

Peter handed them a book that had 'The Moon Wand' written on its cover in a beautiful hand. It was a leather bound book with the title embossed in gold.

'You have no idea how magical your necklaces are,' said Rose. 'You will understand their power by and by. Remember, this book is banned in the kingdom and anyone who is known to possess it will be punished. When Merissa found out that she had overlooked this one thing, she banned all books that had so much as a sentence with the word 'wand' in it. She couldn't cast the spell again because that kind of magic is so evil that doing it the second time would, no doubt, kill her. So, please take good care of the book and keep it away from Merissa's clutches.'

'And here is a map of the whole of Catriona,' said Rose, handing Sara a map. 'You will need it.' She went on, 'You must be wondering how we have these things. These two things have been the properties of the royal family for a long time. Your mothers gave them to us for safekeeping towards the end of their rule. It was your property placed in my custody, to be handed to you when you arrive in Catriona. And that's exactly what we are doing now.'

'Thanks, Rose. One last question. Who was that old man who had come to summon us?' Sara asked.

For a minute, Peter stared at them, astonished. Then, before their eyes, he began to change. He grew shorter and thinner and his face stretched and elongated. Finally in front of them stood the same old man who they had met, with the bumpy nose and black watery bird-like eyes. Only he didn't wear a toga now but the same clothes that Peter was wearing a moment ago. They were two sizes too big for the old guy.

'Did you—are you—so you were—!' Sara stammered hopelessly.

'Yeah. Peter *was* the old man who came to summon you here. He can change his appearance whenever he wants. I must say, Peter, that's a neat piece of magic!' Rose said appreciatively. 'Catriona is the birthplace of magic, by the way. Almost everybody here has magic in their blood. Some choose to use it beneficially but some use it for evil. Even *you* have magic in you.'

Oddly enough, neither Sara nor Crystal was too surprised to hear this. Somewhere, deep down, they had always known they were different. Now that she thought about it, Sara could remember several incidents when her powers had gone out of her control—always in cases of extreme anger or sadness.

She remembered one such incident from middle school when her maths teacher, Ms Sweetpea—that was her name—had been particularly cruel to her.

That week, Sara had scored high in her maths test and she was happy. As she examined her paper for the few mistakes she had made, a paper ball hit her head with a soft thud. She ignored it.

Soon another hit her, then another. Finally, overcome with frustration, Sara threw the paper ball back at Stella—the class snob. Stella immediately stood up and drawled in her whiny voice, 'Miss! Sara's throwing paper balls at me!' And in spite of Sara's spluttered explanations, Ms Sweetpea had walked over and deducted five marks from her paper.

She remembered the hot tears that had splashed on that test paper and a growing feeling that something inside her was itching to get out. She remembered looking hard at her paper without registering anything. The feeling gradually grew till it became so overwhelming that she gave way to it, and to her horror, the test paper burst into flames in her hands. She yelped and leaped up and everyone stared at the burning paper. A moment later the flames had subsided, leaving her palms unscathed, with only the ashes of the charred paper in them. After that, she had had to do the unpleasant work of explaining to Ms Sweetpea, the principal *and* her mother why she had only the ashes of her test paper. She remembered being surprised at the strange, almost proud, expression on her mother's face when she had broken the news to her. Since that day, everyone in her class called her 'Fire Girl'. Many stayed away from her, perhaps scared of her.

'Earth to Sara! Hey! You there?' Crystal was snapping her fingers in front of her face and Jasmine was barking madly.

'Yeah! I'm fine! Relax!' Sara assured them.

Something occurred to Crystal: 'Hey, hey, hey! Wait a second! We have been, and will probably be, here for a long time. Won't anyone at home miss us?'

'No, my dear, when you are here, time stands still in the human world,' Rose replied.

'What do you mean, 'human' world?,' Crystal asked, a little defensive.

'Oh, the world where people who don't have any magic at all live—in short *your* world,' Rose replied and Crystal nodded.

Suddenly they heard the sound of boots crunching on the gravel outside. Someone was coming towards the cottage.

'You must go now,' said Rose, hurriedly. 'They should not see you here. We will handle the rest.'

Sara, Jasmine and Crystal slipped out through the back just as they heard the guards knock on the front door. 'Is anyone here besides you two?' one of them asked Peter.

'No, who are you looking for?' Peter replied calmly.

'Are you sure?' asked another guard, suspiciously.

'Lucas, Neil! Why don't you join us for some cookies and milk?' Rose intervened, quickly taking out a tin of cookies.

As they came in and started eating, Sara and Crystal quietly slipped away.

~

As soon as they were well away from the palace and consequently, from Peter and Rose's house, Sara took out the book and opened to the first page. On it was written—

To make the Moon Wand is not an easy task. You must go through many trials and make many sacrifices. Gather the four stones that are the four shades of blue.

'Great, just great,' said Crystal sarcastically.

Sara turned to the next page:

For the Aquamarine gem:

Soldiers use it for self defence
Think hard, it is common sense
Somewhere in Catriona you can go
Somewhere between two that is low
Not something that you can hold
Let the magic unfold!

'It's the same everywhere, isn't it? No philosopher, Prophet or "magician" will ever write something simple or at the very least, understandable!' muttered Crystal, shaking her head.

'But it has to lead somewhere,' Sara, looked equally puzzled.

Crystal, ever practical, took a deep breath. 'Okay. Let's take this step by step. See, for one thing it says here that it is a place in Catriona.' Crystal took out the map and started reading the names aloud: Mashinalavae Hill, Honey Grove, Whitewood

Jungle, Silver Armour Mountain, Valley of Ordnance...

She paused for a moment. Then she cried, 'That's it! Silver Armour Mountain is the place! "Soldiers use it for self-defence"! Says a lot about their naming of places though. Silver Armour Mountain, *so* creative!' Crystal mocked.

'Woof, woof!' barked Jasmine approvingly.

Sara peered over her shoulder at the map and drew in her breath sharply. Then she slowly shook her head.

'No. It's not Silver Armour Mountain. But before I tell you my theory, I need to confirm it. Give me that backpack.'

Crystal slipped it off her shoulders and passed it to Sara. She held it high out of Jasmine's reach to stop her from reducing the soft straps of the backpack to slimy, half-chewed ribbons. For a minute, she rummaged in it pulling out some broken pieces of potato chips in the process. This, apparently, was not what she wanted. She tossed them carelessly behind her, cursing under her breath. Jasmine jumped up delightedly and gobbled up the chips.

Finally she found what she wanted: her iPod. Curious, Crystal peered over Sara's shoulder and watched Sara flip through the multiple screens till she stopped and pressed on the Dictionary application.

'Dictionary? Really Sara—,' started Crystal.

'Shh! Just watch,' Sara replied.

She typed in the word 'ordnance' in the search box.

'Wait a sec! How on earth does your iPod work here, anyway? asked Crystal, ignoring Sara's quelling looks.

'Well, as long as the apps don't need Wi-Fi, they'll work, because the program has already been fed into the memory of the machine,' Sara replied patiently.

They peered at the screen at the results that had come up for the word 'ordnance'. They were:
1. Mounted Guns
2. Military Equipment

Sara gave a whoop of triumph and jumped up.

'The place where we need to go is the "Valley of Ordnance". Silver Armour Mountain can't be the place because it is a mountain. Mountains are high but the poem says that the place we need to go to is "low". "Somewhere between two that is low", remember? So it can't be a mountain, it has to be a valley. "Ordnance" means military equipment, which is obviously used for self-defence! And it's also an area or a place in Catriona, just like in the poem! See? It fits perfectly!'

Crystal stared at Sara for a moment and then gave her a hug. 'You are a genius, Sara!' she said. Jasmine barked in agreement as if to say *I knew that all along! Don't tell me it took you so long to figure it out!*

'So what are we waiting for? Let's get going to the Valley of Ordanincey!' exclaimed Crystal.

'Ordnance.' corrected Sara but Crystal waved her hand dismissively.

'Yeah, whatever.'

Sara looked at the map again. 'According to the map, to reach the Valley of Ordnance we have to travel *away* from the palace. We need to travel through the Water Spirit Jungle and it looks like it will take us three days to reach there, judging from the distance.'

'That was fast,' said Crystal, admiringly. 'Now we need some food and water. Let's go back to Rose's house.'

Darting through the bushes, they reached Rose's house

and crept in through the back door.

'Hey Rose and Peter,' they whispered. 'Are the guards gone?' Their whisper was loud enough to startle both of them. They turned around in a hurry. Rose stifled a scream of surprise. 'What are you doing here? Why are you back?'

'Listen, I just thought of some more questions,' Crystal said, ignoring Sara's groans about getting to the point. 'How do we go back home when all this is finished? And why are we doing this? Why *us*?'

Sara sat down on a beanbag, thinking how valid Crystal's questions were.

Rose sighed and sat down heavily beside Sara. 'See, I'll be honest with you. I can't guarantee that you will go back home. But your mothers are—if you are able to rescue them—skilled in inter-realm travel. Only very skilled magicians can do that and I have a sneaking suspicion that the Moon Wand, if you manage to assemble it, can help you get home. And you,' said Rose, putting her hands on each of their shoulders, 'are our princesses.'

'Yeah, yeah. But apart from that, give us one reason why we should do this?' said Sara, harshly, and immediately regretted it.

Peter suddenly got up, grabbed Sara by the shoulder and yanked her harshly to her feet. She was so surprised that she couldn't protest. He dragged her to the window roughly and forced to her to look outside.

'Hey! Wha—!'

Peter silenced Crystal with a look full of sadness and uncontrolled anger.

'Look! See outside!' Peter cried, his voice thick with emotion.

Sara looked out. The scenery was beautiful. Lush green meadows stretched everywhere and modest huts and palm trees dotted the fields. People were working in the fields. They were thin and pale and their faces looked sad.

'See?' screamed Peter. 'Cheerful faces that used to always wear smiles, have been replaced by grime-streaked skeletons with dead eyes.'

Sara carefully observed everything that was going on in the fields in front of them. Every field was being watched by a group of strong, fit men in shimmering red and gold uniforms and the insignia of a serpent eating its own tail stitched in gold thread on their front pockets. They wore heeled boots with sharp spurs and a long scabbard hung at each of their waist. A long whip was held, dangerously poised, in each of their hands, their faces were set, and their eyes, hard. Everyone was working, from ten-year-old children to the elderly, their thin bones struggling to keep them standing. The animals around them stumbled and limped, many of them had been injured by the soldiers for their amusement. Sara recoiled as she heard the crack of the whip on an old woman's back. The soldiers' high, cruel laughter rang out...

'What do you say now, dear princess? This is Merissa's rule! Catrionians have to work and give all their harvest to the queen! Thousands of people drop dead every single day not only because of exhaustion but also because they have simply lost the desire to live! There is no famine or drought but what does that matter? They are still dying and are at the mercy of the queen's soldiers! Do you still want a reason why you should defeat the witch Merissa? This is *your* kingdom Sara!' Peter turned his face away, furiously blinking away tears of anger. After a moment's pause, he turned around, gazing steadily at Sara. 'And scores of people are being hunted down Sara, you know why? Because they support your mothers. They are cruelly hunted down and slowly and painfully killed, while their family members are forced to stand and watch .'

'But *you* can make this right Sara,' Rose said softly. 'I know that we shouldn't force this upon you but we have no choice. Your mothers wanted to raise you in the human world, away from all this enmity. Why? To buy you time so that you can cultivate your magic and one day return to save Catriona. But you seem to have got used to your perfect life there,' Rose turned away, brushing away a solitary tear.

'We do NOT have perfect lives! Do you get that?! We never had! Our mothers disappeared when we were little. We manage our studies alone, stay alone and do everything alone! When people ask us where our mothers are, what do you think we say? We say they disappeared and are possibly dead and then they cluck their tongues sympathetically and offer their condolence! What about our fathers? Oh we never knew them at all! All our lives people have either mocked us or pitied us. Perfect life? Why don't you give our life a go and see if it's perfect?' Crystal shouted, her face livid. Everyone was taken aback, even Sara had never seen Crystal in such a rage before. ' Perfect life, indeed!' Crystal muttered again to herself as she stormed up and down the room.

Jasmine sat whimpering quietly through all this conversation.

Sara took a deep breath. 'I'm sorry,' was all she managed to say.

'Hmph...me too,' said Peter and Crystal together.

'And I want to tell you something else,' Rose said nervously. 'They—Merissa ki—'

'Rose, not now. It would be too hard on them,' Peter warned.

Crystal's eyes narrowed and Sara asked suspiciously, 'Tell us what?'

'Nothing, nothing,' Rose said, hastily.

'I have been dragged into this kingdom, almost got caught by guards and have just flown into the most murderous rage ever. You might just want to answer the question,' Crystal answered, a hard glint in her eyes.

Rose didn't say anything.

'Where are our fathers?' asked Crystal suddenly.

'I didn't want to upset the two of you,' started Peter.

'Too late.'

'Well, Merissa killed…' Rose couldn't bring herself to say it.

'…your fathers,' completed Peter just as Rose burst into tears.

Crystal looked like she'd been smacked between her eyes. Even Jasmine whimpered. Something inside Sara snapped. All her life she had been mocked and ridiculed because she had had no one to look after her. She had no real friends except Crystal and Kyran. And now all of a sudden she had just discovered that her one consolation—that fact that she had known everything about her mother and that they were very close—had been ripped away from her. And finally, this weird, psychotic murderer of a queen had captured their mothers and killed their fathers.

Almost instinctively Sara and Crystal turned towards each other.

'We're going!' they chorused, their bodies rigid with wrath. Peter and Rose stared at them.

'All this time I have been wondering why we should even go on this…this stupid…quest!' Crystal said, stammering a little. 'But now we know why we're going,' she nodded at Sara.

'Yeah. We're going on this insane journey to avenge our fathers and rescue our mothers, and also to put that evil witch Merissa in her place! Yes Rose, we're going and don't look at me like that,' Sara continued, still looking as if she would like to throw something.

'But Sara…you do realize right that your mothers may not still be…' Rose gulped fearfully, '…alive.'

Sara gave a wry smile. 'I get it, but that's all we have to hold on to, right? The fact that they are still alive.' Neither Rose nor Peter had a reply to that.

'Coming back to what we originally came here for, can you give us some food and water for our journey?' Crystal asked, looking at them hopefully.

'Of course,' said Rose. Then she paused. 'I hate to see the daughters of our beloved queens like this,' she added in a low, sad voice.

Peter put his hand on her shoulder. 'Why don't you look at it this way?' he said. 'How lucky we are to have the daughters of the queens back amongst us! They are the most courageous people I have ever seen—and the prettiest!' he said, grinning.

'You're right, we *are* lucky,' Rose smiled as Crystal and Sara blushed faintly at the praise. She rushed to the kitchen and was back in a moment. She opened Crystal's backpack and stuffed a packet of food and water into it.

'I didn't know you used plastic here!' Sara exclaimed.

'You know, Sara, we are not exactly uncivilized! We do use plastic but haven't been confronted by the problem of pollution because *we* take care,' said Rose with her hands on her hips. 'You better get going now,' she added.

As Sara snapped her fingers to rouse Jasmine from her nap, Peter stepped forward. He grasped Sara's hands in his own and shook it heartily.

'I'm sorry,' he whispered. Sara smiled and went to hug Rose.

'You won't get into trouble because of us, right?' Crystal asked as Peter shook her hand.

'I don't think so. Unless, of course, you go around telling people that you visited Peter and Rose's house when you first came here,' said Peter, his eyes twinkling. 'But if we do get thrown into jail…' he shrugged. 'It's just two more people on your rescue list.'

Crystal's eyes danced. 'You can definitely count on us to save you!' she winked and hugged Rose.

Jasmine barked joyously and gave Rose a lick and insisted that Peter pet her. She then walked up regally to stand between Crystal and Sara.

'By the way we should warn you that—,' Rose started to say but then clamped her lips shut.

'What?' asked Crystal and Sara, together.

Rose shook her head and the girls decided not to push it. They waved goodbye to their new friends.

'Bye, Rose! Bye, Peter! And thanks for everything,' shouted both the girls, waving as they went out through the back door.

'Okay, so let's get this over with and rescue our mothers and then go home! Tell you what? As soon as we finish all this, we'll have dinner at my house—pizza. I miss it already.' Crystal said, smiling, as they walked toward their destination. She deliberately left out the topic of their fathers from their conversation.

'Yeah, you're right. But you are paying for the pizza!' remarked Sara.

Crystal laughed.

'And we could rent that new horror movie too.' Sara added.

'Uh-huh,' said Crystal her legs already aching. 'I don't think we need more horror in our lives, what with a disappearing family, a mentally unstable queen and a psychotic magical sister!' she said grinning.

Sara punched her playfully.

'Ow! Merissa won't know what hit her till it's staring at her in her ugly face!' Crystal said.

'Yeah, yeah! The declaration of intent is all very good but it would really help if you could move those legs of yours!' said Sara, running ahead.

Laughing and joking, they walked towards their destination as the sun sunk lower into the horizon, staining the sky blood red.

∽

5

'Wake up!' cried Sara into Crystal's ear. 'WAKE UP!'

Crystal sat bolt upright.

'Got it, got it I am awake,' she said before Sara could scream again.

Sara grinned. 'Come on, if we start now we will be able to reach the Valley of Ordnance by tomorrow.'

Crystal sighed and got up. In no time the girls were on their way.

Soon the two girls were on the outskirts of Whitewood Jungle. As they entered the jungle, the girls stared in astonishment. There was not a single living tree in the jungle! On either side of them, rows of white trees ran endlessly. The trees were certainly a sight to behold, made of ivory with delicate leaves and chiseled flowers. Every groove on every bark was meticulously sculpted. Ivory birches bent over the path forming an arch above their heads even as the willows and cypresses formed another canopy. Even the sunlight that filtered through the leaves looked white. The whole place should have been beautiful, but instead there was something sinister about the woods. An overwhelming silence cloaked the place and assailed one almost physically. There were no sounds of twittering birds or animals darting around. There wasn't even the barest whisper of a breeze. The soil was a faded brown and the grass had withered and died. The place was completely barren. Through the trees, they could make out the Whitewood River, its azure waters marred by muck and a substance that looked suspiciously like blood. Jasmine whimpered and hid behind Crystal's legs, with her tail between her legs.

They began their trek cautiously, their sense of confidence already failing as they looked at the ominous trees that loomed over them maliciously. Crystal shuddered as they passed a particularly huge tree. Jasmine wedged herself in between their, whimpering pitifully every now and then. She didn't like her surroundings at all.

The girls trudged the whole day with Jasmine in tow, stopping occasionally to rest their tired limbs. But they never waited for long. They hated this forest and wanted to be well away from it before nightfall. The journey was long and tiring but the girls continued on, and the only thing that made them take each step forward was the hope they would rescue their mothers.

Towards evening, after a day-long hike they reached the other end of the forest. Twilight made the forest look even creepier and that didn't improve their mood. Even Jasmine became increasingly irritable. Irked by the girls' slow pace, Jasmine had wandered off ahead of them. But within a few minutes she stopped short in front of a tree. She stood stock still for a moment; head quizzically tilted and then started barking madly. Startled by the sudden barking frenzy, Sara and Crystal raced ahead to where Jasmine was standing.

'Jasmine! Ssh...Ssh. Calm down! It's okay, Jaz. It's just a tree,' Sara said soothingly trying to calm her down.

But Jasmine wouldn't stop. She began barking louder and started backing away.

Crystal squatted down and took Jasmine's muzzle in her hands and forced the dog to look at her. As she looked into Jasmine's dark eyes, she saw they were overflowing with fear, something the girls had never seen before. Crystal took Jasmine in her arms and patted her tiny little head comfortingly. Slowly, Jasmine's breathing slowed and she finally stopped trembling and barking. But the fear didn't vanish. She looked pleadingly at Crystal, willing her to understand what she was trying to say, but Crystal only stared, confused, into her eyes.

Sara had moved a little way ahead to examine the tree which had traumatized Jasmine. She ran her fingers curiously over the milky trunk of the tree. Suddenly she paused. About a millimetre from her finger was an indentation. Sara squinted at it and noticed that it was a symbol carved into the ivory.

'Hmm...a snake, no two snakes,' Sara thought, wonderingly. 'It's Norse...but I don't know what it is. Crystal!' she called.

'Huh?' Crystal came up to her.

'Look at this'.

'Two entwined snakes. Great!' Crystal said. 'I'm sorry but why exactly should I be excited?'

Sara resisted the urge to roll her eyes.

'It's a symbol! Why should there be a symbol, especially

of snakes, carved on one particular tree when none of the other trees have such a thing?' Sara reasoned.

'Oh!' Crystal said, comprehension dawning on her. She examined the symbol carefully. The carving showed two snakes twisted together in an 'S'. One their faces started the 'S' while the other ended it.

'I think I know this symbol! It's from Norse mythology! I wish I could remember what it was!' Sara thought frantically.

As she stretched out her hands to touch it, Jasmine trotted up to them and whimpered.

'I don't think you should—'started Crystal, but Sara had already touched the snakes. Crystal felt a strong tug in her gut and Jasmine yelped. The ground trembled and Crystal just had time to think, *Earthquake!*, before there was a brilliant flash of light and the world went dark.

~

Sara squeezed her eyes shut, overwhelmed with panic. The solid ground dissipated beneath her feet and she felt like she was floating on a cloud. But in a moment another flash of light lit up the inside of her eyelids and suddenly she was whisked back into reality and dropped on to the hard ground.

Crystal and Jasmine lay beside her. Sara got up and offered her arm to Crystal, who took it gratefully and heaved herself up. Jasmine trotted up to them, sniffing disdainfully, with a look on her face that said, *I told you that tree was bad!*

'What *is* this place?' Crystal asked. 'This is *so* not fair! How is it that someone gets to teleport us to Mysteryland?'

Sara looked around, partly in awe but largely in fear. They were on a rocky cliff with several jutting rocks. Behind them was a cave cloaked in shadows. The symbol of the snakes was carved on its outer wall. The sky overhead was dark blue with red streaks. Cries of birds filled the air, bouncing off the rocks, although there were no birds to be seen. A huge pit of boiling lava ran to the right of the cave. In the middle of it was a piece of glowing stone which had something on it that she couldn't make out.

Sara's face clouded over.

'We need to get out of here now. I don't know about you but I don't like this place,' she said.

'Oh sure. And how exactly are you gonna get back to Whitewood Jungle now, considering that we just kinda fell here?' Crystal commented. 'It's a cliff, Sara! There's no way out unless you want to jump.'

'The symbol! Let's touch it again,' Sara said. Jasmine stood beside Crystal, with her tail between her legs, something that was becoming a regular feature of late.

As Sara began to move towards the symbol, a deep voice boomed, 'Too late for that, my dears.'

She jumped back in alarm.

Suddenly a bright light lit up the insides of the cave. Inside were two people.

One was a handsome young man who wore nothing but a thin piece of linen that encircled his hips. He was well built, with a beautiful face and dark eyes framed by a mass of black curls. His dark eyes burnt with bitter anger but they also held a hint of evil mischief. The young man's legs were chained to the ground while his hands were tied to the ceiling by iron chains. But the strangest thing of all was that a snake was fixed on top of his chained hands and it dripped steaming venom. The venom would have dripped down on to the man's face if it weren't for the woman who stood next to him holding a bowl under the snake's mouth. The woman was beautiful in a simple way. She was dressed in a red and grey gown. A long piece of cloth, fastened on to her hair with a silver circlet, fell from her head to the ground. She had a kind face, worn out by tiredness and unyielding patience. Her blue eyes which once must have been full of life were now about as lively as a toothbrush.

'Hello, my dears!' said the man, 'Don't you know who I am, Sara? Ah, Jasmine. You are an indirect descendant of Fenrir! That makes you my hmm…great-great-great grandchild, more or less. How…interesting,'

Jasmine growled. Just then the woman trembled ever so slightly and a sliver of the venom dripped on to his forehead. The man howled in excruciating pain and the ground trembled.

'Hold it still Sigyn! Curse Odin! Even in my resurrected form I have to wait for Ragnarok to be free!' the man bellowed.

'Curse who? Wait for what? Just in case you hadn't noticed, we don't speak Psycho language!' Crystal said with her usual sarcasm, emboldened by the fact that the man was chained. It didn't seem like he could come after them.

'No,' Sara whispered, trembling. 'You can't be! You are—Sigyn. B-b-but—you are dead! Heimdall killed you!'

The man smiled gruesomely and the woman remained still as a statue.

'Ahh! Good! You know who I am. So no need for formal introductions, I suppose? No?' The man laughed mockingly causing panic to rise in Sara's throat.

'Wait! I don't have a clue to who you are and I am betting

that I don't wanna know!' Crystal said, defiantly, wrinkling her nose. 'And I bet you don't know the term 'air fresheners' here? It stinks!'

'Crystal! Shut up! He is really not someone you should fight with!' Sara said urgently.

'Who is this psycho?' Crystal asked, in an undertone.

'Norse,' Sara whispered the word gingerly as if she was afraid that it would bite.

'Which horse?' Crystal asked, utterly confused.

'Not horse! *Norse!*' Sara said, deadly calm.

The man nodded and the woman glanced around apprehensively.

'Loki,' Sara said, choking the words out.

'Isn't that a vegetable?' Crystal asked still bewildered. She couldn't understand why Sara was getting all worked up over an old guy chained to a rock and a woman who was pretending to be a statue.

Sara and Jasmine whirled to face her in unison.

The man chuckled, 'This is getting good.'

'*He* is Loki! *The* Loki! Norse god of mischief! The blood brother of Odin and the bane *and* boon of Asgard! Loki, the shape-shifter, *the* Loki! History, Chapter Three: Northern Europe and its Traditions!' Sara shouted. 'It's not funny anymore, is it?'

Jasmine barked approvingly at Sara's tirade.

'Oh,' said Crystal meekly. 'The Loki who is the brother of Odin, the King of Gods? He lived in their home called Asgard and caused a lot of trouble but he also rectified them sometimes, right?'

'Right. But he killed Balder Crystal, the son of Odin!'

Sara said.

'Yeah. And I was killed by Heimdall, the guardian of the rainbow bridge! God of rainbows, can you believe it?' Loki asked, rolling his eyes. 'Ironic!'

Sara had always had a special interest in mythology. All through school, she had devoured every mythological book she could lay her hands on and as a consequence she had sufficient knowledge on Norse, Greek, Roman, Egyptian and Indian mythology.

So it was no surprise that she knew about Loki and his wife Sigyn. He was a god in Norse mythology who lived in the heavenly abode of the Norse gods, Asgard, where Odin, the king of gods, ruled with his queen Frigg. Initially the gods tolerated him and some, like Odin, even trusted him. The only god who was always suspicious of him and despised him was Heimdall who would, in turn, kill and be killed by Loki. Loki was known for his cruel jokes that sometimes resulted in deaths. He had killed Balder, Odin's son with a spear made of mistletoe. When Frigg, the queen of heavens had heard that her son Balder was getting nightmares of him dying, she went around the world, extracting oaths from every creature to promise not to harm Balder. She got an oath from everyone except the mistletoe which she had considered too small and weak to hurt Balder. And then one day when all the gods were having fun throwing weapons at Balder and enjoying the fact that he never got hurt, Loki made a spear out of mistletoe and handed it to Balder's blind brother Hod. Hod in all innocence threw the spear guided by Loki and Balder fell down dead. As a punishment, the gods imprisoned Loki and fixed a snake on top of him whose venom, when it fell on him, would cause him to writhe so violently that it would cause earthquakes. The most famous of Loki's children were Fenrir the gigantic wolf; Jörmungandr the Midgard serpent, the mythical evil serpent that encircled the world; and the eight-legged horse Sleipnir. According to Norse mythology, there would come a day when the whole world would be destroyed in a great battle called Ragnarok which would take place between the gods and the giants. During this time Loki and Heimdall would kill each other and so would the Midgard serpent and Thor, the god of thunder. Fenrir would kill Odin and in turn, Odin's son Vidar would kill Fenrir. After the battle, the world would be cleansed of all evil and the process of creation would begin anew once the surviving gods were reunited.

All this went through Sara's mind in a flash as she stared at Loki.

Crystal evidently was thinking on the same lines. 'Listen, how are you even alive? Ragnarok, remember? I thought all that history repeating itself nonsense is also applicable now!' she asked.

Loki and Sara both blinked. Sara couldn't believe that Crystal was actually demanding an explanation from a god.

'Hmm...Well I like you—' started Loki.

'Well I don't,' Crystal pointed.

'Dude, seriously, what the hell! Stop talking like that, 'cause I for one do not want to end up dead! Are you *trying* to get us killed?' Sara burst out.

'I seriously don't get why we are scared of the guy in chains.' Crystal said with a genuine note of confusion in her voice.

'Ah, because the guy in chains can do a lot sitting in this dreaded prison of his,' Loki replied. 'I brought you here to convince you of something. I brought you here to convince you to abandon your foolish quest and side with Merissa. She's much more powerful than the older queens! And with you two, she can conquer the earth. My son, the mighty Midgard serpent shall submit only to her and then even your world, where you humans live, shall be annexed to Catriona,' Loki explained.

'You are with Merissa! So you're a *bad* god? Are you willing to give up your family, the Norse gods, to side with Merissa?' Crystal asked, astonished.

'My *family* didn't care one bit for me when I was with them. Upon Thor's hammer, I would love to get even with them. And you see, there is no good or bad. There is chaos and order. There is also power—obtained by any means—and weakness. I, belong to neither. I am committed to none and am owned by no one—'

'He says that like it's a huge honour,' Crystal mumbled.

'—and by nothing. I choose. I side with those who are most likely to win. And this time, I have sided with chaos, with power and strength to condemn the weak,' Loki continued after shooting a dirty look at Crystal.

'But you're not doing it for the sake of glory, are you? There has to be something in it for you,' Sara said irritated.

Loki's eyes lit up.

'I always knew you were smart! Of course there are benefits for me too. Power, like I said, and glory, of course. But also revenge for being condemned and banished from the society of gods. Punished like this and trodden on by my own brethren!

A chance to get even with them. A second chance to live. That's what Merissa offers me. After Ragnarok, all the gods were resurrected back in Catriona because Catriona is the Land Of Myths—where myths come true! Merissa offered me a path of revenge and I took it,' Loki said.

'Wait a minute…are you saying that all myths come alive in Catriona? *All* the gods and heroes?' Crystal asked astonished.

'Yes, exactly. Greek, Roman, Norse, Indian, Egyptian… they all come alive,' replied Loki.

'That's creepy on so many levels!' Crystal shuddered. 'But why will they listen to you? All of them have their own kings and leaders!'

'They shall bow before me! They shall destroy or be destroyed!' Loki shouted.

'Okay, okay, you might have already mentioned that!' Crystal said exasperated of this madman's ranting.

'I thought you gods can never be killed?' Sara asked, puzzled.

'Of course we can be killed. It's somewhat like this. Assuming you kill a god—let's call him God X—assuming you kill X, then X will most likely flicker and vanish or disintegrate into a pile of sand. This means that X has been banished into his mythology's underworld. Like the underworld Niflheim for Norse or the Duat for Egyptian. So they are not dead in the human sense of the term but it will take time for them to re-form and rise up again from the underworld. But eventually they will and that's why history keeps repeating itself. Do you understand?' Loki explained it like he was explaining something as simple as photosynthesis.

'Uh…' Crystal was baffled.

'Oh, so when you fatally wound gods or monsters or even "kill" them, they just get transported into their underworld till they gather enough strength to come back?' Sara was trying to work it out.

'Yes. Sometimes it takes centuries for them to come back but sometimes, it may only take them a few days or even a few hours! It all depends on the method used for their banishment. Like sympathetic magic can expel someone for a long time,' Loki nodded approvingly.

'Sympathetic magic! I read about it somewhere. It's sort of like Voodoo, right? Where you use a replica or piece of something to impose your will on a bigger thing? The more the likeliness between the two objects, the better it works. Is that right?' Sara asked anxiously, with the air of someone who had just finished her assignment and was showing off to a teacher.

'Perfect. Now back to Merissa. She never did realize that it would be me who would actually control her, not the other way. Who told her to capture your mothers? Me! Oh and wait, let me think. That cold December night, who were those extremely troublesome kings in battle who I had to have assassinated?' Loki asked maliciously. 'Ah yes…your fathers.'

A chill spread over Sara as Loki laughed cruelly.

'You, you… coward!' Sara spat at him.

Loki propped himself on one elbow and his face clouded over as Sara spat at him. Crystal's mouth was clamped shut and her eyes had a murderous rage in them.

'What in the world do you want from us?' Crystal asked, her voice deadly calm.

'What I want is for you to leave Catriona and never return. Or you could join Merissa, that is to say, join me,' he said.

Crystal gave a bitter laugh. 'Oh that's rich. Join you, huh? Join you, a spiteful, cowardly, ailing half-dead creature with not a trace of self-respect left in that filthy, mangled body of yours!'

'Watch your tongue girl, otherwise the consequences—'

Sara stomped over until she stood towering over Loki and spat full in his face. Loki recoiled.

Then she turned to Sigyn.

'How do you bear your vile husband?' Sara asked.

Sigyn started to say something but Loki silenced her with a look.

'I suggest you just drop that bowl of poison on his head and leave him!' Sara screamed. She swiped her hand at Sigyn and instinctively, Loki winced. She walked back, satisfied.

'So back to business,' said Loki cheerfully. 'I take it that your answer to my proposal is no?'

Crystal and Sara nodded emphatically.

'Then I'm afraid I have to kill you,' Loki said happily. 'And now that you are going to die, I might as well tell you that there is a way out of here—the same way that you came in!'

Loki sucked in his breath and shouted out the last thing that Sara wanted to hear:

'FENRIR!'

6

Crystal's eyes widened and she gasped. 'No!'

Jasmine let out a long mournful howl.

Sara looked wildly around and said, 'No! It can't be! Fenrir is fettered by that extraordinary leash, what's its name?' she snapped her fingers in frustration. 'Gleipnir! That's what the leash was called and your son, Fenrir the wolf, can't break loose!'

'But you forget my dear, Chaos is stronger!' Loki replied, with a wink. 'I shall rally all the gods and they shall be my servants! Merissa shall serve as my second-in-command, she *is* an amazing strategist. And the gods shall destroy or be destroyed!'

They should have run at that moment. They should have kicked Loki and touched the serpent symbol again. They should have done everything they could to get out of there. Instead, they chose to talk.

'What? You mean Fenrir broke free?! And you're going to start another Ragnarok?' Crystal asked, surprised. 'But doesn't that mean that you get killed *again* by the Rainbow God?'

Jasmine had a wild, deranged look in her eyes. She grabbed hold of Sara's tee-shirt and tugged insistently. Sara pushed her away.

'You could say that. But this whole concept of destroying the whole world doesn't quite appeal to me,' Loki said, spreading out his hand in a business-like manner. 'What I'm going to do is improvise. I *am* going to start another Ragnarok but this time, *I* will choose who survives and who dies! Chaos shall win and I—I mean, Merissa shall rule! The other gods shall be banished so deep into the Niflheim that they won't be able to get back at all. I shall use this improvised Ragnarok to conquer the whole world!' Loki laughed like a villain right out of a horror film.

'This time, I shall have power over every single one of the ancient traditions. I shall be aided by all those gods who have been banished or overshadowed by their brethren and together we shall take over the world. I chose Catriona to start with because Catriona is the very centre of magical energy, the place where magic is created. It's extremely easy to tip the delicate balance between Chaos and Justice provided you have the right people on your side—and who better than the monarch of Catriona? What better place to start than here, the very core of power and the land of gods?'

'But how are you not going to die? Is it another harebrained scheme to attain immortality? Maybe another eternal army or something?' Crystal asked sarcastically.

'Absolutely, yes!' Loki laughed gleefully at her stunned expression. 'You see, the ruler of the realm of death is my daughter Hel! Surely you've heard of her, ruler of the dead!

My beautiful daughter Hel! She will always let me and my army leave her realm unharmed! She will help me rule the nine worlds!'

A strangled gasp escaped Sara.

'Nine worlds?' Crystal asked Sara under her breath.

'According to Norse mythology, the whole cosmos—' Sara started.

Jasmine was frantic now. She ran round and round in the same spot, barking madly till Loki gave her a stern look. She whimpered and went to stand behind Crystal, tail tucked well between her legs.

'What's cosmos?' Crystal asked.

'The cosmos is...well, you can say that it's a fancy word for universe. The Vikings believed that there were three levels in the universe and each had three worlds. So there were nine worlds. On the first level was Asgard which was the world of the Aesir, the main group of gods. They were also called the sky gods. Then there was Vanaheim, land of the Vanir. The Vanirs were the second group of gods and were known for their knowledge of sorcery and magic and for their skills at foretelling the future. And there was Alfheim, land of the light elves. They were considered good omen.'

'On the second level was Midgard, the land of humans; Nidavellir, land of the dwarfs and Jotunheim, the land of the giants. There was also...urgh...I always forget this one... Svar...yes, Svartalfheim, the land of the dark elves. They were...well, opposites of the light elves. On the third level was Niflheim, the world of the dead and Hel, the realm of the dead,' Sara finished triumphantly, forgetting for a moment where she was.

'Well done, my dear!' Loki smiled a dazzling smile.

'Shut up! Sara, that's really great and all but we need to get out of here. Now!' Crystal said, urgently, looking at Jasmine pawing the ground impatiently.

Suddenly, the ground trembled, then stopped, then trembled again.

'Oh no! Footsteps!' Sara said, her panic returning.

'*Paw* steps, you mean,' said Loki .

After that, the girls needed no encouragement. They glanced at each other and instantly came to a silent agreement.

"Jasmine! Run, now!" Sara shouted.

They started sprinting towards the snake symbol on the outer wall of the cave. The ground shook more violently and with it came loud sounds. *Thud, thud, thud.* The wolf was nearing. Sara fervently prayed with all her heart that whatever was coming was not the wolf, Fenrir. All the myths indicated that anyone who meddled with Fenrir would bring upon disastrous consequences on themselves.

'Almost there…come on!' Crystal urged herself on. If she could just jump…

They were still at a considerable distance from the outer wall. Just as Crystal heaved herself forward for a stupendous jump, Sara screamed, 'No!'

But it was too late. Crystal felt herself leave the ground and a huge shadow fell over her.

'Oh God!' she screamed She shut her eyes tightly and braced herself for the painful crash. But with a sickening crack, her head snapped backwards as an invisible force yanked her backwards.

She fell to the ground, right in front of the looming monster.

'Have you heard of the rock Gioll? That's the rock Fenrir was chained to. It is right here, by the way. That's why I was able to transfer my strength to Fenrir so that he could escape. This signifies the start of my Ragnarok,' Loki chuckled.

Slowly, Crystal lifted her eyes to look at the wolf. It was a sight that she would never be able to forget.

In front of them stood a wolf the size of a double-decker bus with mad, fiery red eyes and a snarling, frothing mouth. He had a long, sleek muzzle with pointed ears and beautiful, silver-black fur. As his drool hit the ground, it sizzled and steamed. His incredibly muscled body rippled as the wolf scraped his scimitar-like claws on the rocks. He regarded the two girls and the dog with a malicious amusement and bared his mouth in a gruesome smile. His teeth were strong and sharp, the canines like that of a saber-toothed tiger, tapered sharply to a deadly point. Sara couldn't help but gulp—those teeth could rip her apart to pieces.

Fenrir roared. The blast from it was so powerful that it lifted the girls and Jasmine and slammed them against the rocks.

Crystal groaned. Sara and Jasmine scrambled up quickly.

Fenrir turned to Loki and growled respectfully, if you can say that. They seemed to have a conversation in silence at the end of which Loki replied, 'Kill them. But please, make it interesting. I haven't had this much entertainment in a long time.'

Fenrir then bent down till his head was level with Sigyn's. He gnashed his teeth experimentally, making Sigyn tremble.

Apparently Fenrir didn't like his stepmother very much.

'We need to reach that symbol fast. We don't stand a

chance otherwise; we don't even have weapons, for God's sake!' Crystal whispered, as they watched Fenrir.

'Here's what we'll do. The only place which is relatively safe is under him. We need to find a way to get under him and then we run,' Sara said.

'Fine. Let's do it. Jasmine, stick close to me,' ordered Crystal.

However they never got a chance to execute their flimsy plan as right at that moment, Fenrir turned. He rushed towards the mat full speed. Crystal and Sara jumped out of the way at the nick of time as Jasmine bit Fenrir's leg. He didn't seem to even feel it.

'What's plan B again?' Crystal yelled.

'We don't have one!' Sara replied.

'Great,' Crystal gritted her teeth.

Fenrir barrelled back towards them. Sara had time only to pick up a stone near her feet and as he got closer, throw it at him with all her force.

What happened next, Sara and Crystal could never put in order. All their concentration was on making sure that they didn't get squashed into a grease spot by Fenrir or get burnt by his drool. Without proper weapons, they were forced to use only stones, little use against such a monster. Jasmine too tried to help in any way that she could, biting Fenrir as hard as she could, although it didn't seem to bother him.

'We need to find a way of defeating Fenrir...fast! With him here, there's no way to reach that symbol,' Crystal said, panting. 'How did the gods ever defeat him?'

'When he broke loose during Ragnarok, Fenrir killed Odin and then Odin's son—Vidar—killed Fenrir easily since the wolf was already tired from his fight with Odin! But I really don't think he is very tired now!

'Wha—Move!' Crystal screamed as Fenrir reached out with a giant paw to crush them.

They dived in opposite directions just in time. Jasmine ran under him and bit him in his underbelly, which is usually the softest part of any four-legged animal. But Fenrir apparently was an exception. His underbelly was as hard as his body and though she got a good hold on him, it didn't seem to affect Fenrir in any way.

'Loki's child Fenrir...the gods kept him in Asgard to keep an eye on him...but he grew too large...and they had to restrain him by tying a leash to him. The leash was made by dwarves with eight unlikely ingredients but Fenrir refused to wear it—,' Sara rolled out of the way, panting, while simultaneously picking up a rock.

She threw it with all her might and it hit the wolf square on the muzzle. A gash opened and a sick, green mucus-like substance oozed out, which Sara supposed was probably monster blood.

'—Fenrir refused to wear it until a god—Tyr, the god of war and the bravest—put his hand into Fenrir's mouth as a show of good faith. The gods fettered him but in anger Fenrir bit off Tyr's hand.'

'Yeah, yeah I know that!' Crystal shouted as she bombarded Fenrir with stones.

'Fenrir! Enough of this play! Kill them!' Loki roared angrily. Fenrir bared his teeth and let out a bloodcurdling roar, running towards them, with Jasmine still dangling on to his underside.

As Crystal stood rooted to the ground, Fenrir opened his maw wide ready to swallow her whole. At the same time Jasmine bit harder, finally biting into the flesh. Fenrir's maw closed in a long, howl of pain. With a paw he batted Jasmine aside, who went flying, her mouth full of blood. Fenrir growled and opened his mouth once again to finish Crystal off, his saliva dripping and making the ground smoke.

Sara jumped up and crashed into Crystal, knocking her sideways, just out of reach of Fenrir's snapping jaws. As both of them tumbled to the ground, Sara felt a sharp pain near her elbow and then a sting.

'Whew! That was close. Thanks Sara! Sara? Sara!' Crystal knelt down next to her.

Sara lay curled in a foetal position on the floor, clutching her right arm. She was convulsing slightly. Crystal turned her gently over and gasped. A deep gash ran down the whole length of her arm, cutting through her arm and ending just above her wrist. Black blood flowed out from the wound and Crystal realized with a start that Fenrir's drool, which seemed to be poisoned, had entered Sara's blood through the gash.

'Agrh…ahh…' Sara moaned.

'Ssh..ssh…you'll be okay!' Crystal whispered, tears starting to blur her vision. She ripped out a piece of her tee-shirt and bound it tightly around Sara's wound. It was the best that she could do.

'Listen Sara, stay here. When I distract Fenrir, you grab Jasmine and touch the symbol. There is no other way. I'll…I'll find a way to get back,' Crystal swallowed. As she rose, Sara grabbed her tee-shirt. Crystal turned and saw that some of the old light had come back into her friend's eyes.

'There is another way...Gleipnir...the leash! The leash that was used to fetter Fenrir! We have to tie him to the rock with the same leash! Get it. You know where it is,' Sara gasped.

'But I can't leave you and Jasmine!'

'It's the only way!' Sara said fiercely. 'Go! I'll distract that stupid mutt!'

Crystal nodded and raced at once to the huge pit that they had seen upon their arrival. She leaned out carefully to see what was down below. The pit bubbled with lava and the walls were rocky and hard. At the bottom of the pit was a perfect circular stone and on it lay something, glittering. Instinctively, Crystal felt that it had to be something important. She scanned the area for some sort of ladder or rungs to get down to the circular stone but there was none. She gritted her teeth and wiped her sweaty palms on her jeans. This was where her rock climbing skills came in.

'Hey, you dirty mongrel!' Crystal heard Sara call out. And then there was a thud as Sara threw a stone at Fenrir.

Fenrir roared and charged.

Then for Sara it was a game of tag. Her only intention was to keep Fenrir occupied and to distract him from Crystal and Jasmine. She tried to weave her way through Fenrir's paw to the cliff-side while Loki shouted encouragement to Fenrir.

'Fresh meat, Fenrir! And *royal* meat too! Must be tasty!' Loki called out maliciously.

Crystal in the meanwhile was climbing down the pit, using the crude rock formations as hand and foot holds. But every time Fenrir barked, the vibrations dislodged loose stones that hurtled down into the boiling lava.

'You big mutt! Come and get me!' shouted Sara, picking

up a large pointed stone. She had intended to run between his legs and stab him from the behind. But her strength was draining. Her left hand throbbed painfully from the wound and it was next to useless. She slid between his paws but apparently Fenrir, thought that it was easier to just sit on top of her so he started to squat down with the intention of crushing Sara. She panicked and raised her hands instinctively. The sharp stone in her hand cut through Fenrir's flesh. He rose hurriedly, and keened in pain. That was time enough for Sara to rally her strengths.

Crystal was nearly there. She lowered herself down and leapt lightly onto the rock. Sweat poured down her back and the heat was almost unbearable. She felt like her face would melt right off. She cautiously approached the silver shimmering thing that lay coiled on the floor in a small heap.

It was Gleipnir, the leash. But it wasn't like anything she had ever seen. It shimmered in the light like liquid mercury. It looked magical, but horribly fragile.

'Well, it *has* to work,' Crystal said to herself, 'We don't have any other choice.' Two more steps and she would be there. Crystal reached out and grabbed it.

'Oh man! Ow!' she shouted. A searing pain shot through her fingers. She clutched her hand till the pain subsided and then reached out and touched the Gleipnir gingerly. Nothing happened. She slowly picked up the looped end of the leash and started pulling it towards her. The rope was cool to touch and was silky silver in colour. She pulled and pulled, but she never reached the end. It was as if it the rope was—

'Extendable! Of course. It can be extended till it reaches Fenrir! That's why it can't be removed from this rock, what was its name? Gioll!' Crystal realized. 'Great! Let's start climbing.'

Crystal looped the leash over her wrist and started climbing. As she got closer to the top and closer to the wolf she noticed that it got heavier and heavier, till it was almost too heavy for her to carry. It was hardly noticeable at first, then it gradually increased till Crystal could barely climb.

Sara was still playing tag with Fenrir but he was slowly gaining on her. Finally she was forced to back up against Loki's cave, in between Loki and Sigyn. Fenrir smiled, baring his teeth horribly that sent shivers down her spine.

'Now this is getting interesting!' Loki, noticing Crystal's disappearance, 'Where's your little friend? Hiding?'

Sara was right in front of the bowl of poison that Sigyn held.

'*Poison!*' Sara thought. 'Oh, please work!' She turned around to face the bowl of poison.

'Football, don't fail me now!' Sara muttered and whirled around to face the bowl of poison.

Then she jumped and flipped in the air while kicking her right leg up. Her leg connected with, the bowl of poison and it went sailing through the air, out of the startled Sigyn's hand and emptied on top of Fenrir. Sara landed lightly on her feet after the somersault. Loki and Sigyn stared at her. But Fenrir dropped to the floor howling and shrieking and writhing so badly in pain that the ground rocked and trembled. The rear of the cave started caving in. The venom had burnt through his skin and green blood poured out. As Sara stood back to survey her handiwork a voice shrieked, 'Sara!'

'Crystal!' Sara ran to the edge of the pit, ignoring the rising pain in her arm.

The leash had become increasingly heavy for Crystal to carry as she got nearer to the top. Finally when she was only a few footholds away from the top, the ground had started shaking violently as Fenrir howled in agony. Inside the pit, the walls started giving way. Large chunks of rock broke away and fell into the lava. Crystal could just about hold on to the wall. 'Oh great,' she muttered, dragging herself and the leaden leash upwards. Only two more steps left… only one more…She stretched out her hand to pull herself over the edge. She pressed down with her left hand to pull herself up but the pressure together with the shaking of the ground was too much for the rock. It gave way and Crystal fell, the leash dragging her faster down towards the lava.

'Sara!' she shouted, groping for a handhold along the sides.

With a painful jerk, her bloody fingers caught on an indent and she hung there, a few metres away from the top. The leash was slipping out of her hand but she managed to catch it with two of her fingers and slowly, she inched it over her wrist.

A second later, Sara's face appeared over the edge, beaded with sweat and blood.

'God, Crystal! Typical of you to get into such a mess. Now give me your hand, fast!' Sara screamed, stretching her hand out.

Crystal's face was grim with pain but she extended the hand on which the leash hung with some difficulty.

On seeing the leash, Sara raised her eyebrows and Crystal nodded. She grasped Crystal's outstretched hand and pulled. But the leash was too heavy.

'Fenrir, you mutt! Kill them!' Loki yelled.

Fenrir got up and winced. Then he looked at Loki murderously.

'Oh—I mean, Fenrir, please take care of them, will you?' Loki amended his sentence. Fenrir growled approvingly.

'Come on, Crystal!' Sara said tugging her hard as Fenrir began advancing towards them.

He was only a few yards away.

'Sara wait, don't pull me up yet,' Crystal cried wincing. If she couldn't carry the leash to Fenrir, she thought, Fenrir would have to come to them.

'What? Are you crazy? Dude, I really can't hold on much longer. Besides Fenrir is really getting closer!' Sara shouted.

'Please, just trust me!' Crystal pleaded.

Fenrir was only two yards away…and now, one.

'Pull!' Crystal shouted.

In that split second many things happened together. Fenrir snarled and leaped just as Sara gathered her remaining strength and yanked Crystal up. Crystal used the rock wall as leverage and jumped out of the pit and high into the air, throwing the leash at Fenrir with superhuman effort. It fell over Fenrir's head, and with a snap, yanked Fenrir backwards, dragging him into the pit just as Sara scrambled aside. The wolf fell into the pit, down to the rock named Gioll, so surprised and astonished that he didn't even howl.

For a moment, there was silence. Then Loki screamed—an awful screech that sent shivers down Crystal's spine. As he screamed, the ground started cracking and the cracks snaked their way here and there as fissures opened on the cliff. Sara tried to steady herself but she felt light-headed from her blood loss and exhaustion. 'Come on, Sara!' Crystal grabbed her and ran like she had never run before. She reached Jasmine who was bleeding from several places. Crystal grabbed her too and ran again.

Sara's head was throbbing. Multicoloured specks danced before her eyes. She let herself be dragged by Crystal. In the distance, she could hear Loki shouting and cursing. She could feel Crystal slowing down. She was gasping and panting now. Then suddenly she felt Crystal jump and her hands brushed against the snake symbol. There was a brilliant flash of light and a moment later Sara landed hard on the ground, her eyes tightly shut. She arched her back as a bolt of pain shot through it. Then there was a flash of red and everything went dark.

7

When Sara opened her eyes, she saw that she was staring up at a wooden ceiling. She tried to sit up but her head exploded in a spurt of pain. She clutched it in her hands and fell back against the soft pillows. She gathered that she was lying on a mattress on a wooden floor.

Suddenly she heard a lot of shuffling nearby and Crystal's face appeared in her line of vision.

'Sara! Thank God you woke up! It's been so long! Are you feeling alright?' Crystal's face was anxious.

'I'm okay. Where's Jasmine? Is she alright?' Sara asked. 'And Crystal? Was that place…Fenrir and Loki…were they real?'

'Yeah they were,' replied Crystal grimly, 'and Jasmine's dozing over there,' she pointed and hurried over to prop Sara up with some cushions. 'We are at Sanaya's place. She is the one who saved us and healed you.'

'Healed—,' Sara ran her right hand over her left. It was perfectly smooth. She gasped and looked at her once-wounded hand. She saw no indication that it had once been infected.

Sara turned and saw a woman standing quietly near the doorway. She presumed that she was Sanaya.

She was an old woman of medium height with twinkling grey eyes and a slightly upturned nose. Streaks of white ran sporadically through her hair, barely visible against her pale blonde curls. It was gathered away from her face but a few unruly strands framed either sides of her face. Her face was clear though her age was beginning to show in the wrinkles around her eyes. Her whole face lit up in a peculiar, almost funny way as she smiled at Sara.

She came forward. 'Hi, I'm Sanaya. Healing is my specialty.'

'She rescued us just in time,' Crystal said.

'I found both of you lying on the forest ground. You had fainted. Luckily I found you while I was on my evening walk, otherwise that nasty gash on your arm could have caused trouble for you, Sara. Now I suppose you're hungry? Crystal and I already had dinner.'

'Thanks so much, really,' Sara said, looking around. The room was sparsely furnished with a comfortable looking sofa dominating the area. There was a dining table set on the other side of the room. A few bean bags were all around along with a cream-coloured rug and some light, multicoloured duvets.

Crystal brought her a plate laden with pizza and a bottle of Rio, raspberry flavour.

'Thanks,' Sara murmured and started tucking in. 'What time is it?'

'It's nearing twelve,' Crystal said, nonchalantly.

'Twelve? Twelve! Have I really been knocked out for that

long?' Sara said, suddenly ravenous. She started attacking the food with a vengeance. It tasted just the same as it would have back home. After polishing off the entire pizza, she threw her head back against the sofa, took a deep breath and closed her eyes. She was content.

Her eyes flew open as she heard Sanaya gasp.

'Where did you get that?' Sanaya asked, pointing at her throat. Her finger was trembling violently.

'Wha—oh, the necklace? It's my mum's,' Sara said simply, not wanting to elaborate on the subject.

'Don't you lie to me!' Sanaya's voice took a dangerous tone. 'It was Anastasia's.'

'That's exactly what she is saying. Anastasia and Olivia are our mothers!' Crystal intervened.

'Oh really? Then I'm the goddess of magic!'

'Really,' Crystal said her hands of her hips. 'What's with the sarcasm?'

'Can you prove that you are their daughters?'

Sanaya was very direct. She didn't believe what the girls were telling her.

'You want us to prove if we are their daughters?' Crystal burst out, angrily. Tears were welling up in her eyes yet she had that fierce angry look. 'I'm so tired of proving ourselves, being pushed around, forced to take up this stupid world-saving quest! After staying motherless for so long somebody comes and tells us that they are not dead after all! And in spite of that a daughter can't be taken on her word when she claims that a certain woman is her mother! No, we have to *prove* ourselves.'

'Yes! You do! And I'll not have people going around saying

that they are the queens' daughters! Take back your claim or get out of my house,' Sanaya shouted back at Crystal.

Sara thought hard. She was nervous and her head throbbed. How could they prove that Anastasia and Olivia were their mothers? What if they weren't able to prove it? 'No', she thought, shaking her head vigorously in an attempt to clear her thoughts, 'Think with a clear head and you'll find the solution to every problem on earth' was what her mother always used to say.

'Can't you just see the likeliness? They gave us these necklaces and they brought us here to this world!' Sara said.

'Okay. If you are really their daughters and are from the human world, then tell me how long has it been since they disappeared from your world?' Sanaya asked.

'Ten,' they both replied without hesitation.

'*Well!* You'll really are the princesses!' Sanaya gasped.

Sara unhooked her necklace and handed it to Sanaya who took it reverently and sat down on the floor cross-legged. Her eyes filled with tears.

'Are...are you okay?' Sara asked, hesitantly. Her own eyes were moist and she bit her lip to hold back her tears. Yet they managed to escape and rolled down her cheek. She stole a glance at Crystal. She was crying too.

'Yes Sara, I am,' said Sanaya. 'Your mothers were great women...'

Then she burst out crying.

Crystal walked up to Sanaya and said, 'I am really sorry I shouted at you.' Sanaya nodded.

'Me too,' she said. Then she wiped her eyes and said, 'I'll tell you how I knew Anastasia and Olivia. Please sit.' Sara and Crystal sat down hurriedly. Sara quickly gulped down her last piece of pizza and Crystal drained her glass of juice. They desperately wanted to hear what Sanaya was going to tell them.

~

'Let me start,' Sanaya said, handing a mug of hot chocolate each to the two girls. The clock chimed twelve times. It was midnight and the girls were sitting around Sanaya's fireplace. After the food, Sara had felt a lot better and now she was sat on one of the bean bags with a duvet on top of her. Crystal had pulled the cream rug against the sofa and was sitting on it, propped up by cushions with a green duvet spread out on her lap. Sanaya settled down on a brown cushion beside them and began:

'Long long ago when your mothers and I were young girls, we were the best of friends. We did everything together. The only difference was that they were, of course, royalty and I was only an ordinary citizen. But they were always kind and humble and never let me feel any different from them.

'Anastasia and Olivia were twins and there was always a question in everybody's minds about who would eventually ascend the throne. They were the children of King Theodore and Queen Yasmine. Their parents had a very tough time choosing the heir to the throne. Olivia and Anastasia were alike in almost everything and it soon became apparent that each was as capable as the other. Finally after many meetings and countless disputes, it was decided that both Anastasia and Olivia would be the heirs and rule Catriona together. That is how Catriona came to have two queens.

'After their parents' deaths, when they became queens, they built a separate house for me very near the palace and appointed me as the head healer of the kingdom. This was a very prestigious position as the head healer was in charge of all the healers of Catriona and reported directly to the monarchs. The gift of healing is very rare, and the queens insisted that everyone treat me with respect. They would come to me for assistance and even made me a part of councils on the welfare of Catriona.

'Once, the identical necklaces that they wore broke and the queens were heartbroken. It was an heirloom, passed on from generations of Catrionian monarchs. I fixed it for them. My siblings—I have a brother and sister—too went off to serve the queens in the palace.'

'How did Merissa come to live with them?' Crystal asked.

'I was coming to that,' Sanaya replied. 'Once, when the sisters were hardly a few months old, their parents went on a tour of their kingdom. They would do that regularly to make sure that all was well in Catriona. They stopped at a seaside town. After spending the day with their people, the two of them went on a boat ride deep into the sea. As they sailed out, they came across a wicker basket floating in the water. It had colourful markings on top, and the queen, curious, asked for the basket to be hauled up into the boat. When they brought it up, they were surprised to see a newborn baby girl inside it. They brought the child, only a few weeks old, back with them and named her 'Merissa' which means 'of the sea'. Merissa was brought up by the king and queen with their own children—Anastasia and Olivia.

'At that time, it was customary for the royal children to

have a nanny or a nurse of their own. Merissa was brought up by a nanny who secretly nursed a grudge against the king and the queen and hence against Anastasia and Olivia too. And because your mothers were close to me, the nanny poisoned Merissa's mind against me too. Thanks to the nanny, Merissa grew up with the idea that her foster sisters were evil and power hungry.

'As time passed and Anastasia, Olivia, Merissa and I started spending time together, we noticed Merissa get more and more jealous of the princesses. Eventually, all of us got married: I to Peter, Anastasia and Olivia to the brothers Cedric and Andrew and Merissa to Willam. The kingdom passed smoothly into the hands of your mothers. Merissa was very unhappy about that. Anastasia, Cedric, Olivia and Andrew ruled Catriona wisely. But there was a small twist in the tale. Although Merissa was evil personified, her husband was the very epitome of kindness, wisdom and grace. The queens were fond of William and gave Merissa and William a part of the kingdom to rule.

'But Merissa was not satisfied. She wanted the whole of Catriona to herself. Slowly and clevery, she hatched a plot to assassinate the two queens. I didn't pose any immediate threat to her in her goal for the throne, so I was left alone. When William came to know about the plans, he was horrified. His loyalty towards Catriona was stronger than his love for Merissa. It was he who sought out your mothers and told them about his wife's murderous plans.

'The queens immediately ordered that the title of 'queen' which had been conferred on her be taken away. She was stripped of her titles and relegated to the life of a commoner.

Queen Merissa went back to being just Merissa.

'However, the compassionate queens ordered that a house be given to Merissa to live in, and some money, even though she was a traitor. They also allowed William to rule her kingdom. When William returned to his kingdom, after telling the queens about Merissa's plans, Merissa acted as though she regretted her behaviour.

'An hour before she was due to leave the palace, Merissa asked for a last meal with William. Little did William know that it would be his last meal! Merissa went into her chamber to get a bottle of wine. She laced it with a few drops of deadly poison. An unsuspecting William drank it all up. The next moment, he fell off his chair and lay on the floor, writhing in pain. Then, with the suddenness with which it began, it ended. William stopped moving and lay still on the floor. Dead. Merissa had heartlessly murdered her own husband. Later she summoned her maid to spread the news of his death and started weeping inconsolably. She *did* put on an amazing act. The rumour was confirmed when the maid was found dead the next day.

'The queens on hearing of this felt sorry for her. In the ensuing mourning for William, Merissa's treachery was forgotten and she was allowed to continue reigning her kingdom in William's place.

'No one spoke any more about the incident, and after a few months, Anastasia and Olivia gave birth to their babies, Sara and Crystal. Now the kings and queens started going more frequently to the human world. Anastasia and Olivia strongly believed that the human and magical worlds needed to know more about each other. They also wanted their babies to be comfortable in both worlds from a young age. This was the opportunity Merissa had been waiting for. She sent her trusted maid to work at the palace and earn the trust of the royal family. The maid did as she was told and very soon, she became a trusted aide.

'Once, the kings and queens had gone to tend to some matters of the state leaving both of you with the maid. Merissa seized the opportunity and had the treacherous maid deliver both of you to her.

'When the kings and queens came back home, they found their children missing. When they asked around, they came to know that they were last seen with the maid, who had said that she was taking them for a walk. They hadn't returned since. The royal family was powerful. They had magical powers which they put to good use. They also had a strong bond of love and telepathy with the two of you. It was not difficult for them to find out that both of you were in the clutches of Merissa in her palace. The queens were frantic. They couldn't attack the palace or threaten Merissa in any way for fear of Merissa harming you. In the end, they decided to go meet her and reason with her.

'The four of them disguised themselves, put up strong magical wards around themselves to protect themselves from any trouble and travelled to Merissa's palace. She met them outside. She had archers positioned on the battlements and she herself radiated with black magic, the kind that was banned in Catriona and that the royal family had never suspected she indulged in. She held both of you in her arms and demanded that your fathers and mothers remove all their protective enchantments and wards. Fearing harm to the two of you, the family quickly removed their wards and stood defenceless in front of Merissa. As soon as Merissa was sure that there were no more wards, she shouted, 'Now!' Two arrows whizzed down from the battlements and hit Cedric and Andrew squarely on the chest. They were not wearing any armour and the arrows were poison tipped. The kings fell down dead.

'The queens were distraught. They wrung their hands in anguish and cursed Merissa but they couldn't harm her because she still had both of you in her arms. Merissa only laughed.'

The temperature in the room seemed to drop. Sanaya's voice choked as she looked up and saw Crystal clutching her duvet in a valiant attempt not to cry. Sara's eyes were unfocused and her face was wet with her tears.

'I'm...I'm so sorry!' Sanaya wrung her hands.

'Forget it. We know about it,' interjected Sara, still looking devastated.

'Yeah, let's not dwell upon it. It's not gonna help,' Crystal dug her fingernails harder into the duvet. Although they had known that their fathers were dead, hearing it again didn't make the blow any less painful. 'Just continue with the story,' she said, slowly.

Sanaya stared at them for a moment, then she nodded and continued.

'After much pleading and cajoling Merissa proposed a deal—she would return the children to the queens, if they would leave Catriona. She also demanded that in four years' time both of them would have to come back to Catriona and live as prisoners. Merissa knew that Anastasia and Olivia would not go back on their word. The queens pleaded with her to let them come back after eight years. Merissa granted that plea. Your mothers wanted eight years because they wanted you to grow up knowing your mothers and have a stable childhood till you were eight.

'Once the pact was reached, Merissa released the two children.

'The queens returned to the palace with the two of you. However, before they went to the human world, they came to me and advised me to go somewhere else. They expected Merissa to come after those who were the favourites of the two queens. I couldn't say no. So I came here to Whitewood jungle and built my cottage.'

'Wow,' said Crystal softly. 'This kind of explains....' but she was cut short by Sara.

'You said you had a brother and sister,' Sara said, looking hard at Sanaya. 'The ones who went to work in the palace.'

'Yes,' Sanaya said.

'Are their names Peter and Rose by any chance?' Sara asked, excited.

'Why, yes!' Sanaya replied, a little surprised. 'And I am pretty sure it's not a coincidence that you know them'.

'We do know them. They were the first people we met in Catriona. In fact, Peter was the one who summoned us here in the first place! They know our mothers too. They told us lots of things...' Crystal gushed in one long breath.

'And they were the ones who started us on this impossible quest,' finished Sara.

Sanaya looked at them curiously. 'Would you mind telling me why I found you both in the forest, hurt and dirty?'

Sara and Crystal looked at each other and then recounted their adventures at Loki's lair. As they spoke, Sanaya's eyebrows crept higher and higher and when they finally finished, she let out a big sigh.

'These are troubled times, and though I always knew that myths came true here, I have never known the gods to make themselves the centre of attraction like this before!' she said in a troubled voice.

The old clock on the wall above the fireplace struck one.

'My, my... look at the time! It's well past midnight! Now off to bed, you two!' Sanaya said, getting up.

'Just one last question please...' begged Crystal.

'Fine, go ahead.'

'Um... we are on our way to the 'Valley of Ordnance'. But you know the place where the tributaries of the Whitewood River meet? Well it kind of forms a water body so huge that we don't know how to cross it,' said Crystal.

Sara turned to look at her in surprise.

'How do you know that?' she asked.

'You were knocked out for more than three hours, remember? I went for a walk, with Jasmine. I didn't really see much but I could make out the outlines of a water body glittering in the distance and figured it was where the tributaries met,' Crystal said casually.

Sara nodded. She went to sit beside Jasmine and stroked her while she slept. She had been most helpful that day.

'I don't really know how to cross that place, but I do know that to get to the crossing point you have to seek permission first,' Sanaya answered without hesitation.

'Oh thank god! I was expecting something extremely difficult! Who do we have to seek permission from?' Sara asked happily.

'The tree, of course!' Sanaya replied.

'Oh, I'm sorry,' Sara laughed. 'Sorry, I thought you just said that we need to ask permission from a *tree*...'

'But my dear, that's exactly what I said!' Sanaya answered patiently. 'See, the place where the cliff begins is marked by a white dogwood tree. The White Dogwood is the only living tree in this forest. You must go to it and treat it with great respect. It can grant you access to go beyond the woods. It may ask you some questions too. There is no way you can cross the sea without seeking permission from the tree. Now if the Dogwood does give you access to Merlandia—the land of Merlandians—you move on to the edge of the cliff. I don't know what happens after that, really,' said Sanaya. 'Now off to bed you both. You have a long day ahead.'

Sara and Crystal didn't protest and went quietly to bed.

Curled up under soft warm blankets, Sara said, 'Honestly, I don't think I'm going to sleep at all tonight.' But she was asleep even as soon as she closed her eyes. Crystal took a little more time to drift off. She was mentally going through all that had happened that day. She prided herself on her stamina and even though she refused to admit it, the day had done enough to sap her of strength and break her tough exterior.

8

Early the next morning the two girls and Jasmine set out towards the Dogwood tree. Sanaya had packed some lunch for them. It didn't take them too long to reach their destination. The sight that welcomed them was extraordinary. Sara and Crystal couldn't help but stare with open mouths.

The tree was huge with a thick dark brown trunk and sweeping, widespread branches. The white branches were dusted with flowers and spread out in all directions. Every few minutes a few petals would free themselves from the branches and float lightly down on to a white blanket of petals below. It was such a relief to see an actual living tree in the ivory-tree jungle.

Sara was the first one who gathered herself and addressed the tree, albeit a little nervously: 'Um…Mr…I mean Mrs…I mean, sorry! Can we please see you Mr, Mrs, or Miss Dogwood! We…um…have to go across the sea and as all of us know, it's not possible without your help. So please, you know… like…could you help us? Please?'

'Dude, you sound so confused!' Crystal said, raising an eyebrow.

Nothing happened. The leaves rustled in the wind. Both of them looked around cautiously. Then Crystal tried, 'O Mighty Dogwood!' she began, 'Please come to our aid as without your will and permission we cannot cross the sea. Please appear before us!'

'Wow! You said that so well!' Sara looked at Crystal in admiration.

And still nothing happened. 'Okay, I give up,' said Crystal. 'What does the Dogwood think of himself? And how do we know if this myth is real? Sanaya could have just made that up! How can we trust her?'

'Well, duh! She did know all about our mothers!' Sara said, but Crystal could tell that she was frustrated as well.

'I'm so going back to Sanaya and asking her. We can't wait here endlessly.' Crystal said.

The leaves of the Dogwood rustled again. 'Shssssssss,' they made a pleasant sound.

'I wish the tree would just speak instead,' Sara thought out loud.

'They're talking!' Crystal was beginning to get excited.

'I swear I heard something too', said Sara, as the leaves continued rustling. She looked up. A strange shape had appeared at the top of the tree. She did a double take and looked closely. Was it a girl sitting on the tree? 'Can't be,' thought Sara to herself and looked up again. Indeed, it *was* a girl. Her skin was so pale that it seemed almost translucent. Her wavy auburn hair was piled up high above her head.

'Who *is* she?' wondered Sara. Her violet eyes and her long flowing white gown added to the mystique. She was as white as the dogwood flowers and they could hardly make her out through the white branches. No wonder we didn't see her, thought Sara as she quietly touched Crystal's arm. 'Don't say a word, just look up,' Sara whispered to Crystal. Crystal looked up and gasped.

'Aaahh!'

'There! Sophistication goes right out of the window,' Sara muttered. The girl heard the muffled scream and looked down.

'Hello!' she said shyly.

'Hello. My name is Sara and she's Crystal', said Sara stepping forward. 'Who are you?'

'I am a treseren—a tree spirit. My name is Vereshia.'

'I think um.... Are you the one we're supposed to meet and seek permission for going to Merlandia?'

The girl smiled. 'Yes. But for that you have to answer my riddle,' said Vereshia.

'Fine,' Sara and Crystal shrugged.

Vereshia raised her hand and pointed at something in the directions of the girls. It didn't take Sara and Crystal much time to realize what she was pointing at. Sara subconsciously raised her hand to touch the stone-less necklace that each of them wore.

'Ah! I see you wear the necklaces,' Vereshia said. 'You are of noble birth then. I don't think this should be very difficult for you.'

The girls looked at each other wondering what Vereshia was saying. They could sense the nervousness on each other's face . If they messed this up, they would never be allowed to move on.

'It's okay,' Crystal said. 'Remember, it can't be too difficult a riddle to solve. We are destined to move on…don't worry. We'll get the answer…' the confidence in her voice belied the nervousness that was stamped on her face.

'Alright,' announced Vereshia, to get their attention. 'Here's your riddle—

'A place where my face meets my body

But my neck cannot be seen,

A place where man cannot reach

Which is my face, which is my body and which is the place?

You have three tries. If you ask for help, it will cost you one try.'

'A place where my face meets my body but my neck cannot be seen, a place where man cannot reach,' Crystal repeated. 'Maybe the face is the space, the earth is the body and the meeting point is the atmosphere!' And before Sara could stop her, Crystal had told her answer to the treseren.

'Wrong,' said Vereshia and began humming a tune.

'Man can reach the atmosphere, idiot! What were you thinking?' Sara growled to Crystal.

'I think we should take the hint.' Crystal nodded.

'We'll take the hint,' said Sara. Vereshia smiled,

'Fine, then. Where does the sun disappear?'

'Erm…the sun disappears into the sky? The earth? No, wait…the horizon!' exclaimed Sara suddenly. 'That's the answer.'

'What are you doing?' hissed Crystal. 'Let's discuss this before you spurt out the answer. We only have one chance left.'

'It's logic, not magic! When the sun sets, it seems to disappear behind the horizon! The face is the sky, the body is the earth and man can never reach the horizon, can he?' Sara reasoned.

Vereshia smiled. 'You have done well, my little children,' she said. It seemed strange, thought Sara, to be called 'little children' by someone who looked so much younger. 'Horizon, indeed, is the answer.'

Sara looked at Crystal. 'You can close your mouth now, it's the right answer!'

Crystal broke into a smile. 'Dude!' she said. 'You *rock*!'

'Now there's more that I need to tell you,' said Vereshia, her voice taking on a serious tone. 'When your mothers were the queens of this land...'

'You knew our mothers?' Crystal interjected.

'Yes, of course, everyone here knows you and your mothers. Please don't interrupt.'

'Sorry.'

'When your mothers were the queens of this land,' Vereshia began again, 'there also lived a famous philosopher named Oractess who had the power to foretell certain events in the future. Oractess once went to your mothers and told them that Merissa would soon try to capture Catriona—yes I know that you know about the prophecy, Crystal, but please do keep quiet—for herself, but your mothers had great faith in Merissa and paid no heed to what Oractess had to say. He also foretold that two young princesses from the outside world would come to rescue the kingdom. He knew that to obtain the Aquamarine gem, they would have to pass through here so he gave me this to give to you.'

If Oractess himself had given her whatever-it-was he had given her, thought Crystal, then exactly how old was Vereshia? She opened her mouth to ask her this, but then thought better of it and shut up.

Vereshia then opened her fists. In each of her palms was a medium-sized flower. The girls gasped, for they were the most unusual and beautiful flowers they had ever seen. One was a beautiful shade of blue-green while the other was a breathtaking violet. At the centre of each flower was the most perfectly cut and polished diamond! Sara and Crystal gasped in surprise.

'That's not all,' Vereshia said. 'He told me to tell you that *"Concentration is the chief weapon for all magicians."'*

'Weird,' said Sara.

'Yeah, I know, weird!' Crystal agreed.

'Now you better get going,' said Vereshia.

'Hmm...can't you tell us anything else?' the two pleaded.

'I'm sorry, children, but no,' Vereshia had already started disappearing amongst the branches and the girls could hardly see her any more.

'Wait!' Crystal called out. 'Will you share our lunch?'

Vereshia smiled, 'Thank you, but no!' she said. 'I don't eat your kind of food,' before she disappeared completely.

Sara had completely forgotten about lunch! Now that Crystal had mentioned it, she realized how hungry she was. They settled down to eat.

~

The sun was up but the air was still chilly, especially because they were near the sea now. Sara wandered a little ahead rubbing her arms for warmth. The breeze gently tugged at her hair.

'Concentrate, concentrate my dear child,' the wind seemed to be saying into her ear.

'Huh?' thought Sara. Winds weren't supposed to speak. She shook her head as if to clear her thoughts. Suddenly she felt a cold hand brushing the back of her neck.

'Wear your necklace, my dear,' said the wind.

Sara turned in a jiffy. 'Mom?' she called out. Maybe she was hallucinating, she thought, but the wind had sounded just like her mom.

'Mom! Mom!' She called out again. 'Where are you? Are you there? I want to see you!'

The wind spoke again but the voice had changed. 'Hello Sara,' it seemed to whisper, 'I see you recognized the voice. So you do remember your mother.'

'Who are you?' Sara asked, surprised by her own courage.

'Hmmm...Straight to the point, just like your mother.'

'Who are you and why are you here? And why did I hear my mother's voice?' asked Sara again.

'Wait, little niece, wait,' rustled the wind.

'Niece? Wait a second! I want answers! Why are unknown relations popping up now?' Sara asked, indignantly.

'Before you decide whether I am lying, answer me this: where's Jasmine?' the wind asked.

The question caught Sara by surprise. 'Huh? Jasmine? She'll be here somewhere. She'll come when I call her.'

Sara whistled. But Jasmine did not come bounding out of the bushes. She whistled again. Still no Jasmine.

'What have you done with Jasmine?' Sara asked, her voice

trembling, a little with fear but mostly with rage.

'Nothing! On the contrary, I have her with me now,' said the voice. And to her surprise, Jasmine materialized out of thin air, not on the ground but floating in mid-air! With all her paws up in the air and body pointing towards the ground, Jasmine looked a pitiful shadow of her enthusiastic self. Sara's jaw dropped open.

'Sara,' the wind whispered, 'Had you not been so busy with Vereshia, you would have noticed that Jasmine had been exploring the place on her own. When she reached the cliff, she leaned over a bit too much and lost her footing. Lucky for her, I was there and caught her before she could fall into the water!' said the wind.

Sara was shocked. She knew she would have been inconsolable if Jasmine had died. At that moment, she didn't care who this person or this...thing...that had called her niece, was. She was only thankful to the person for saving Jasmine's life.

Just as she was thinking this to herself, something even stranger happened. Behind the floating Jasmine there materialized a woman. Her eyes were a striking violet. She wore denim knee-length shorts and a lavender top. She was absolutely stunning.

Seeing Sara gaping at her she said, 'Nice style, huh? I always keep in touch with the latest in the human world!'

'Did you just...' started Sara, struggling to finish the sentence.

'...materialize out of the air?' finished the woman. 'Well I *am* the wind! What else would you expect?'

Sara shook her head and rubbed her eyes. When she

opened them, the woman was still there.

'Whatever you are, wind or earth, I don't care! I'm really thankful to you for saving Jasmine's life and that's all that matters to me. Thank you. Thank you very much,' Sara was overwhelmed. 'But tell me...why did you do it? I don't even know you.'

'Because you are my niece,' said the woman, tucking a loose strand of her hair behind her ear.

'Huh?' asked Sara.

'Well, if I am your father's sister, that makes you my niece, girl.'

'Wa-wait a second, you knew my father?' asked Sara, stunned.

'Well, of course!' said the woman, playing with her necklace. 'I was his sister, wasn't I? His elder sister, actually.'

Sara noticed the small charm hanging from a silver thread around her neck. Like the woman, the charm too was delicate. It was a mixture of silver and grey with a touch of black. The design was very intricate. At first Sara could not make out what the charm was, but as she squinted, she could make out that it was four horses pulling a chariot.

'Cool necklace!' said Sara.

'Thank you,' the woman replied airily.

Suddenly Sara remembered the voice of her mother. 'So um...Aunt, er, Wind, where did my mother's voice come from?'

'Oh please don't call me Aunt! It makes me sound so old! Call me Welna.'

'But I thought that you were the wind,' said Sara, beginning to like this lady.

'To the people, yes, I am Wind, but to my relations,

especially my nieces, I'm Welna.'

'But...how did you find me?' Sara asked suddenly.

'Well you aren't really keeping a low profile in Catriona are you? Word about your meeting with Loki has already leaked out. So I knew that you'll were in Catriona and after all I am the Wind! It was easy to find you after that!' Welna said smiling.

'Okay,' said Sara. 'Now tell me about my mother's voice.'

'Oh yes, your mother...' Welna started but was interrupted by an ear-splitting scream. She dropped the floating Jasmine who landed nimbly on the ground. She barked and thumped her tail vigorously against Sara's leg.

'Crystal!' cried Sara going pale. 'That was Crystal!' She turned and ran in the direction of the noise with Jasmine and Welna behind her.

But Crystal was nowhere to be seen.

Sara stood there, nervous, wondering what to do. Then she heard the scream again. The shrill voice was definitely Crystal's, she was sure of it. But this time it came from somewhere deep inside the forest. Without stopping to think, Sara sprinted into the woods with Welna and Jasmine behind her.

∽

9

'Crystal!'

Sara burst through the trees into a small clearing. The entire clearing where she now stood had been transformed, as if magically, into a cold and frozen world—it was snowing and the ground had disappeared underneath the fallen snow. Frost had painted the trees white and icy winds blew around them. Sara shivered in the freezing temperature. Crystal stood right in front of her. But she was with some very unwanted company.

In the middle of the clearing stood a woman. She was tall and thin, built like an athlete, and was dressed entirely in white. A white fur coat covered her shoulders and she wore white snowshoes. A white belt, with the buckle in the shape of a snowflake stretched around her shapely waist and crystal hoops hung from her ears. A white corded bracelet lay on top of her milky white skin. Her long silvery hair was braided into a neat plait that hung over her shoulder, interwoven with spherical opals and with bubblegum pink highlights streaking through it. Her hard, icy blue eyes met Sara's gaze unflinchingly, devoid of all mercy. They surveyed everything around with a half-mocking, patronizing glint. As she moved, snow seemed to flow out from beneath her. Circling her feet was a white Arctic she-wolf with silky fur and razor sharp teeth. Crystal stood at one side of the clearing, apparently as astonished as Sara and Jasmine.

Sara knew what Crystal was thinking: '*Not more wolves!*'

Jasmine had begun to growl ferociously. The woman looked at her coolly.

'Shut up,' she said. Her cold, harsh voice cut through the air like a knife.

'Hey, Ice Woman or whoever you are! You have no right to—,' Sara started to say but the woman flicked her finger and Sara's legs slipped from beneath her and she landed with a bump on the ground. The woman bent and said something into the she-wolf's ear. It nodded and disappeared in a puff of smoke.

'W-W-What on earth…?' Crystal stammered.

'I ordered her to return to its home. They are my sacred animals, you know. She was just here to intimidate you!' the woman answered.

'Well, it certainly worked,' Crystal mumbled.

'Hello, Welna!' said the woman, now addressing Welna, 'How are you? I haven't seen you in a while.'

'Skadi. Why are you here?' asked Welna, her voice deadly calm.

Crystal came to stand beside Sara and mouthed, 'Who is this?'

'Aunt.' Sara said in an undertone. 'We just met!'

'*Aunt?*' asked Crystal bewildered.

'She's our fathers' elder sister!' Sara said.

'Good to see you, too!' Skadi said, mockingly. 'Where are your manners, Welna?'

'Skadi, just let us go! We don't wish to cross paths with you!'

'"*We don't wish to cross paths with you.*"' Skadi mimicked. 'Don't worry, I just want to talk to your dear nieces!'

'Wait! Who are you, and Welna, how do you know her?' Sara asked.

Before Welna could reply, Skadi extended her hand to Sara.

'Hello, Sara. Nice to meet you. I must say you have caused quite a stir in Catriona! I am Skadi, wife of Njord. You must know me...don't you?' Skadi continued matter-of-factly as Sara shook her hand.

'Hey! *I* know you! You're the daughter of that giant who stole those golden apples of youth!' Crystal snapped her fingers in comprehension.

'Thjazi! That was his name! He was the only giant who had the courage to do something like that! Those spineless shadows that you call gods are nothing but cheaters, liars and selfish dogs!' Skadi's eyes flashed with anger.

Something stirred in Sara's memory. Vaguely remembered the story of a giant—Thjazi—who had stolen the golden apples of youth from the goddess Idunn just to spite the gods. But then the gods tricked him and he had died trying to get the apples back.

The skies thundered. 'Skadi, you are angering Thor, it's

never wise to do that!' Welna warned.

Skadi threw back her head and laughed.

'Anger Thor? Oh, he's the only one who has a little self-respect left! All the other "gods" are cowering in their princely homes!' Skadi spat on the ground in contempt.

'Listen, I don't know who you are and what you want from us. It's obvious you are a goddess!' Sara said.

Skadi snapped her fingers and a chair made of ice appeared. She sat down on it and crossed her legs.

'Let me tell you my story!' Skadi started. 'But first I think you should know that I am on Loki's side.'

'What!' Sara burst out. 'You can't...he...he is trying to kill us all!'

Skadi leaned forward and Sara saw the fire burning deep inside her icy blue eyes.

'How would you feel if someone murdered your father? But you already know that feeling, don't you? I feel the same way because the gods murdered my father! Then when I demanded compensation, they made me choose a husband from one of them by looking at their feet! I got Njord, the sea god, as my husband, when I was in love with Balder! You think that's fair? The sea god and the mountain giantess as husband and wife? I was miserable! We finally parted ways because I couldn't stand the sea and Njord couldn't stand the mountains! They ruined my entire life! And you still think I should support those weakling gods? I am the goddess of snow and winter and I can be mild and comely but I can also be harsh to get what I want!' On that alarming note, Skadi stopped.

Sara and Crystal were horrified. After hearing what Skadi

had said, they were left wondering if all the 'good' gods were actually good or not. Welna's face, however, was grim and expressionless.

'You are both bright and gifted. Loki himself admits that and I recognize it too! Do you really think that the heroic gods are as benevolent and kind as they're made out to be? They have all performed many dark deeds but they have hidden them well. Only Balder and perhaps Thor are the better ones! Join me and we shall make sure that everyone gets justice,' Skadi's eyes burned with passion.

'Shut up! Just shut up! You are going on about how you lost your father. Do you have any idea who killed my brothers?' Welna shouted, looking Skadi in the eye. 'Loki! It was Loki who masterminded their assassinations!'

For the first time, a look of uncertainty crossed Skadi's eerily beautiful face.

'Loki?' she asked, surprised.

'Yes! And wasn't he the one who masterminded the death of Balder as well?' Welna asked angrily.

'Wasn't Loki the one who led your father into the trap that the gods had laid to kill him?' shot Sara.

Skadi went limp suddenly. 'Balder's death…Father's murder…I…I had forgotten about that—,' she started. Then suddenly her eyes cleared and she growled, 'Loki! You eraser of memories! You broke the oath that you swore to me!' She then tilted her head as if she was listening to something far off.

Suddenly Sara and Crystal collapsed to the ground, writhing in pain and clutching their heads even though Welna remained standing.

A high frequency screech pierced Sara's and Crystal's ears

and they screamed. Welna, however, remained standing. She tilted her head and looked alarmed. Then a booming voice shouted in their heads, 'Skadi! Make this quick! They are brainwashing you! Stop falling into their traps and get the job done! Yes, I erased your memories! So what? I erased only the painful ones!'

Skadi jumped to her feet.

'I…am…not…your…servant!' she growled. 'Loki, show me some respect! I shall not have you taking my memories away from me!'

But the voice had gone silent. Sara's head throbbed.

'Since when did he learn to mass communicate?' Welna asked as Sara and Crystal picked themselves off the ground. They were still shivering form the cold and the pain and Jasmine had curled herself into a ball. She was the only one who had not been affected by what had happened.

'Listen to me, I do not wish to kill you because I do not want to hurt strong women like you! But Loki is going to win this war and even if I want to stop it, I cannot!' An enormous change had come over Skadi. Her anger was now masked by centuries of sadness.

'I can't do anything now; Loki has me in his control. He had instructed me to get the necklaces from you but…let's just say that I'm not going to do that. However, I have to leave behind some enemies for you to fight, that's the price of your lives,' Skadi said.

All three of them were stunned at Skadi's sudden change of heart and for the first time, they understood the depth of her love for Thjazi and Balder.

Skadi leaned down and petted Jasmine. 'You have the

heart of a wolf, Jasmine. I bless you!'

She put her hand on Jasmine's forehead and her palm glowed. When Skadi withdrew her hand, in its place was the image of an icy blue snowflake.

'I bless that you shall be twice as powerful as the alpha male in a wolf pack and you will be the most powerful in winter or while fighting any creature of the cold.'

'Balder is dead, isn't he?' Skadi said suddenly, and after a few moments, she started weeping but instead of drops of water, tiny pieces of frost fell out of her eyes.

She collected them in her hand and pressed them together. When her hands opened, she held a glowing orb in them. She handed it to Welna.

'Keep it, my friend. With this you can call me for help when you are in trouble. It may cost me my life but I'll do this…for Balder.' Skadi said.

'Skadi, I cannot thank you enough…' Crystal started.

'Thank me by defeating Loki and returning his filthy essence to the depths of Hel!' Skadi's eyes flashed.

'Skadi…why is Merissa doing this? How are Loki and Merissa connected?' Crystal asked suddenly.

'I suppose you know that Merissa hated your mothers ever since her childhood? Loki is drawn towards hatred like a magnet, he always has been. And Merissa's hate was so powerful that Loki decided to use her to succeed in his own plans. That's why Loki secretly taught her the deepest and most forbidden of dark magic. He was the one who kindled the spark of evil in her until it grew into a burning fire. He whispered into her mind ways to capture your mothers and to kill your fathers. He promised her rewards of wealth and power and finally she was completely under his control. Now it's only a matter of time before he takes her as his human anchor,' Skadi said.

'Anchor?' Sara asked, puzzled.

'A god's powers are limited unless they merge with a human counterpart. But that will spill so much magical energy that it could burn the anchor alive. If Merissa becomes his anchor then together both of them will be unstoppable,' Skadi said. 'But I must leave now,' she ended hurriedly. 'Try to not get yourself killed!' she shouted before she vanished in a whirlwind of snow. And with her, the cold and the frost in the clearing disappeared, leaving only a single mound of snow.

Welna's eyes filled with tears as she looked at the misty orb in her hand. 'She'll be miserable with Loki! Skadi would never obey anyone unless they are holding her to ransom of threatening someone who is dear to her!'

'How do you know her?' Sara asked as Jasmine sniffed the leftover pile of snow.

'I am the wind, Sara. Wind and Ice get along well together. I met her one evening in winter, we had dinner together,' Welna smiled.

That sounded so absurd to Sara that she almost laughed out loud.

'Hey Crystal, we haven't really met yet but I'm your aunt! You can call me Welna.'

Crystal nodded.

Welna waved her hand lazily and a gold chain materialized in front of her. She threaded the orb through it and clasped it around her neck.

Sara suddenly became aware of the flower Vereshia had

given her. It was in her pocket. She had forgotten all about it but now it felt as if it was burning right through her pocket. 'Ouch!' she shouted, taking the flower out. She checked her pocket to make sure there were no holes. No burn marks either. Then she stared at the flower in her hand. 'So pretty... my favourite colour...' she said dreamily, murmuring to herself.

Welna's voice cut through her thoughts. 'Where did you get that?' she asked sharply.

'The treseren of the Dogwood tree, Vereshia, gave them to us. Crystal's flower is blue-green,' replied Sara. 'Some guy called Oractess gave it to her and told her to give it to us.'

Welna smiled, like she was remembering an old friend. 'Oh! He thought of everything, didn't he?' she said to no one in particular.

'What do you mean?' Crystal asked.

'Have you two ever fought with real weapons?' asked Welna.

'No!' Crystal and Sara replied, astonished.

'Hmm,' Welna mused. 'Then I guess your reflexes are yet to open up.'

Welna chanted something like a spell and held out her hands. Silver dust exploded in both her hands. She opened her fists. She was holding two intricately carved, delicate silver bracelets. In between each of the silver straps were silver flower pendants. There was an indentation in each pendant, as if a stone in the pendant was missing. Welna put one of the bracelets in her pocket.

'Crystal, please give me your flower,' she said, holding out her hand. Crystal handed her the flower. Welna held the bracelet in her left hand and the flower in her right. She closed her eyes and once again chanted a spell. She gently pushed the items upwards. They flew up. Then they stayed where they were, suspended in mid-air.

For a moment nothing happened. Suddenly, the blue-green flower burst into flames. It burnt for a moment or two and extinguished itself. Now the flower was smaller. It moved forward, towards the bracelet and fitted itself into the pendant. It was a perfect fit! A shower of silver dust exploded around the pendant. It settled in the tiny spaces between the flower and the pendant, sealing in the flower. Welna stretched out her hands. The bracelet immediately fell into her hands. She gave it to Crystal. It felt comfortingly warm on her skin. Crystal clutched it and instantly felt a burst of energy flood her.

'Your turn, Sara,' said Welna. Sara handed her the flower and Welna repeated the process for her. Sara fingered the bracelet fondly. Her's and Crystal's were identical, except the colour. 'These are your enchanted bracelets,' said Welna. 'They enable you to turn them into any weapon of your choice. Wear them. Try them out if you wish.' They both wore their bracelets. Sara concentrated on a sword and Crystal on a bow and arrow. They felt their bracelets growing hot and saw them unhooking themselves from their wrists. There was a burst of light which made them shut their eyes and when the two opened them again, in front of them was a sword, a bow and a quiver full of arrows, hanging in mid-air. They reached out slowly and caught their weapons.

'Wow!' said Sara, sliding her finger along the sharp edge of the blade. The blade was smooth. The hilt was made of silver, patterned with intricate carvings and studded with glittering purple gems. Crystal was also examining her bow.

It was made of oak, sturdy and beautifully carved, inlaid with multi-coloured gems. Her arrows were extremely sharp and well-made and every inch looked lethal.

'These arrows are fletched from the feathers of the magical swans of Catriona. It will be a pleasure to handle them.' Welna said.

'Oh I can't wait to use them!' said Crystal. She had taken archery lessons back home as part of her sports routine. She turned and saw Sara was admiring her sword. She loved sword-fighting even though she had never done it herself. She had spent hours watching movies with sequences of sword fighting in them and committing the complicated manoeuvres to memory...

'Uh, Crystal? I think you may get a chance to use them pretty soon, we have company!' Sara's voice rose. Jasmine yelped and leapt back. All of them turned and looked in the direction where Sara was pointing. The mound of snow that had been left after Skadi disappeared was multiplying rapidly and out of each mound a demon was rising. They were made of ice with carved eyes, mouth and nose and each of them had two pairs of hands that held diverse weapons—an ice axe, a sword, a javelin, a lance, a spear and other weapons that Sara didn't recognize. In no time, a dozen of them sprang up in front of them. Their icy faces were smooth and hairless but a single horn grew from their forehead, like a unicorn's.

'This is not good,' Crystal mumbled.

'No, this is bad. Weapons out girls, this may get nasty!' said Welna.

Sara hesitantly clutched her sword and Crystal drew her bow and nocked an arrow.

The ice demons were advancing upon them.

'Listen Welna—' Sara started.

'I know, I know! You have never fought before, but there's always a first time, right? Your parents were great fighters and this is in your blood! Your reflexes will open up. Ever felt like you can't concentrate on something?' Welna asked.

'Art! I just can't concentrate on my drawing, after sometime my vision starts going blurry and watery,' Sara said. 'Is that normal?'

Welna nodded. 'Things that require a lot of concentration, especially things that you don't like, are tough for you because you can't concentrate. But in battle your senses will be tingling and you'll be perfectly balanced, focused and instinctive,' Welna explained. 'Crystal, do you have anything that you can't concentrate on?'

'Uh...Geography?'

'Nah, that's just plain boring!' Welna cracked a smile. 'Now just trust your instincts and charge!'

Welna's own weapon—a beautiful broad sword blazing with blue fire—materialized in her hands.

Jasmine crouched down, ready to attack. Then, with a ferocious howl, she leapt up and fell upon the demons with a vengeance

As the nearest ice demon reached Sara, she raised her sword clumsily just in time to block the strike. She tried to counter with a thrust but her movements were slow and sluggish.

Crystal shot arrow after arrow at the enemy but they just shattered against their ice bodies.

Welna was duelling with a huge ice demon that had a

double-edged axe in his hands. She managed to duck his blow, slid between his legs and jabbed him from behind. The ice demon shattered into a pile of snow.

Jasmine fought like a wolf, inspiring awe and fear. Skadi's blessings had begun to take effect and soon Sara could only see a blur of teeth and claws as Jasmine bit and ripped and fought her way through the demons. She tore out their arms, scratched their bodies and bit off their legs.

After finishing off five ice demons single-handedly Jasmine stood panting. She was blessed to be more powerful than the lead wolf of a pack but she still got tired. Welna turned to Sara, 'Sara, stop thinking!'

'Excuse me?' Sara replied, fending off blows as best as she could, 'I think I'm still a little busy trying to stay alive!'

'I mean, let your reflexes take over! Stop thinking about what you are going to do and just go with what your body tells you!' said Welna and added, 'Instinctively!'

Sara stole a quick glance at Welna and her eyes widened. 'Turn!' she shouted.

Welna turned and raised her sword just in time to counter the axe of an ice demon that had re-formed from the pile of snow. The weapons clashed and sparks flew. Immediately the demon disengaged and backed away.

Jasmine yelped in surprise as five demons that she had destroyed re-formed around her. She tore them to pieces, but they grew again, from the snow. She clawed away their faces, but still they came back. After the third round, Jasmine was covered in sweat and was panting heavily.

Welna's eyes widened.

'Fire!' she shouted. 'Use fire!'

'Where exactly do we get fire from?' asked Crystal who was still shooting arrows hopelessly at the demons while Sara whirled around the demons, twisting and turning and bringing death with every strike. But the creatures always reformed and Sara, like Jasmine, was getting tired.

'Magic!' Welna replied breathlessly. 'Imagine fire! Set your sword and arrows on fire and then attack!'

'Your sword is on fire. Why is it not helping?' Sara asked.

'It's blue fire! It's cold fire! You need proper fire!' Welna said.

'Easier said than done!' Sara mumbled.

'Concentrate, both of you! Jasmine and I will cover for you,' Welna moved in front of them.

'Why can't *you* do it?' Sara asked confused. 'You are the wind, aren't you?'

'Exactly! I am born into a particular branch of family which is wind and thus my powers are only limited to it,' Welna said, twisting a sword from an ice demon's grasp as she knifed him through.

Sara took a deep breath and concentrated, not on fire but on heat. She really didn't expect the plan to succeed but there was no harm in trying. She began remembering all warm things, things that had fire and heat in them. She thought about the time her mother would bake her cookies, when she was young, and in her excitement to eat them, she would gobble them up fresh out of the oven and burn her tongue. She thought about how she loved to lock an empty room on a scorching hot day for several hours and later, when she opened the room, the blast of hot air that would hit her in the face. She remembered how the soles of her feet heat up whenever she played outside with Crystal, barefoot in summer. Flashes of the day her test paper had burst into flames—in her hands glided past her. She even fondly recollected those days in the sun when she and her mother would go for a picnic in the woods and how they would dance on the wet grass, reveling in the warmth of the sun. She concentrated on everything that was associated with heat and fire. Her body started growing uncomfortably hot, and finally she couldn't stand it. She opened her eyes and almost dropped her sword in alarm.

A tiny flame flickered at the tip of her blade. Sara noticed that she was panting and her forehead was beaded with sweat. She felt as if she had just run a marathon. As she calmed herself, the flame began to grow steadily until the blade of her sword was ablaze. Sara's eyes felt heavy and she was exhausted. But there was no time. She shook her head and held up her sword, ready to get back into the field of action.

Crystal, however, was still struggling with her fire, still concentrating with her eyes closed and gripping her bow.

'Crystal! Concentrate! Try using your emotions to build up your energy!' Welna instructed as Jasmine jumped up and bit off a demon's head.

'God, I really can't—,'

Just then, a demon lashed out at Welna with his sword, leaving a deep gash on the side of her arm. Blood gushed out as Welna shouted out in pain.

Crystal's face flashed with anger when she turned and saw Welna injured. The fierce desire to fight came rushing back to her. Her breath came out in ragged gasps and she focused all her rage on to the arrow that she was holding. She felt her body grow hot and her bow trembled in her hands.

Sara gasped. 'Crystal! Stop whatever you are doing right now! Dude you are steaming! You'll burn up!' Sara shouted thoroughly startled.

But Crystal couldn't stop. She felt her body becoming unbearably hot but she couldn't do anything about it. Her anger flared and she started seeing red spots. Suddenly, on an impulse, she drew out two arrows from her quiver and with trembling hands, shot them at the demons. The arrows burst into flames in mid-air and hit an ice demon on the forehead, stomach and thigh. He shot Crystal a look of surprise, and with an agonizing howl, slowly melted into a pile of steaming water. His brethren, suddenly infuriated, attacked the girls and Jasmine with renewed vigour. Welna shot an approving look in Crystal's direction and Sara looked at her in admiration. But Crystal was drained. She felt nauseous and her head throbbed. But she gave them a big smile and said, 'Let's go kill some demons, shall we?'

Welna smiled but Sara looked at Crystal with concern.

'You sure you're okay?' Sara asked anxiously. Crystal nodded weakly and Sara turned away, still not convinced.

They saw Jasmine and Welna trying to fend off the demons themselves and immediately joined them. Sara stabbed one with her flaming sword. Jasmine set about barking and snapping, preventing any ice demon from sneaking up on the girls as they fought. Crystal shot three arrows together that hit another unfortunate demon right between its eyes. 'Bull's eye!' she said, pumping her fist in the air as the demon melted into a wet puddle. But the joy masked the exhaustion which was slowly seeping into Crystal's body. Sara too was beginning to tire. She was still a bit disoriented with magical energy but this wasn't the only thing that threw her off track. She staggered as a huge wave of nausea washed over her.

The magic was sapping their strength.

Finally, Sara delivered the last death blow to the last ice demon with her fire sword. Now only a huge puddle of water remained, a marker of their great battle.

~

'Proud of you, girls,' Welna beamed at them as the girls and Jasmine trudged to where she stood watching. Jasmine, utterly exhausted, curled up beside Sara to take a quick nap.

'Thank you, but you could've warned us that magic makes you this hungry,' Crystal's tummy rumbled loudly. Her body was burning and her limbs aching, but she didn't want to mention that.

'Hey, I just remembered! *How* are we gonna cross that water body?' Now that the demons were taken care of, Sara struck her forehead with her palm which caused such a sound that it made Jasmine leap up barking. When she saw that she had been rudely awoken when there was no evident threat to anyone's life, she shot a dirty look at Sara and began dozing again.

'Oh yeah! I had totally forgotten about that!' groaned Crystal.

'Girls, girls! Why fear when Welna's here? I'm not leaving my nieces so soon. I'm going to come with you on this thrilling quest.'

'*Murderous.* On this murderous quest,' Crystal corrected. Welna winked.

She then ripped a piece of cloth from her top and tied it to her bleeding wound. She winced as she tightened the cloth over it. 'No more magical energy left for healing,' she explained a little breathlessly.

'Now, about food. When you're with me, you do everything in style!' Welna said, smiling mysteriously.

She unhooked her charm necklace and placed it on the ground. Sara swayed dizzily but Crystal caught her and steadied her. Her magic had cost her more energy because she had to maintain the flame on the sword while Crystal, in the time span when she switched arrows, had just that brief interval to gather her strength. She turned her attention to where Welna had placed her necklace on the ground. There was a momentary flash. In the place of the silver charm necklace stood a majestic chariot. Jasmine, roused by the light, opened one eye quizzically and then apparently realizing that things were about to get interesting, shook herself awake and went up to sniff the chariot.

'W-Wow...' said Sara, shakily.

But before anyone had time to admire the chariot, Crystal's eyes suddenly widened in fear and surprise.

'Er...Welna...?' She was tugging at Welna furiously to look in the direction that she was pointing in.

'What is it?' Welna asked with a twinge of annoyance as she turned to look in the direction that Crystal was pointing at. 'Oh...I see. That could be a problem.'

Sara turned too. 'Aaah! What the hell are you waiting for? *Run!*' Sara jumped into the chariot. Welna seemed to consider the situation for a moment and then scrambled into the chariot too, with Crystal behind her.

Considering the fact that a gigantic fifty-foot ice demon had just reformed from the puddle of water swinging an enormous sword, running away seemed like a really good idea.

10

'What is that?' asked Crystal breathlessly. She was already exhausted and wasn't sure she could fight any more.

'I don't understand. I'm guessing that this is one of Skadi's tricks. She would have enchanted it to reform as soon as all her demons were dead. The only problem is that I have absolutely no idea how to defeat it,' Welna said as she got into the chariot and took the reins.

'How encouraging,' mumbled Sara. She was massaging her throbbing temples with both her hands. 'Whose side is Skadi on, that confused goddess?'

'That's the price of our lives! Skadi could not just leave us free because Loki's oath would bind her from doing so—that's why this obstacle,' Welna mused to herself.

'Calling this giant an obstacle—that's an understatement,' Crystal grumbled.

The only one who seemed completely at home in this bizarre situation was Jasmine, probably thanks to Skadi's blessing. She growled menacingly at the ice giant. The giant bared his stalactite-like teeth and growled back at Jasmine. He had a smooth round head and eyes that were a blur of ice and frost, twinkling with malice. He started moving forward. With every step he took, the ground trembled and the chariot shook. His breath was like ice, freezing everything in its vicinity.

Welna cracked at the reins. It sounded like a sudden clap of thunder and for a moment, Sara's ears popped and she felt a strange pull in the pit of her stomach, the kind of feeling that one gets sitting when an aeroplane takes off from the tarmac, the moment of weightlessness that you feel when in a rollercoaster as it goes into free fall. Jasmine growled a little in discomfort. Sara shut her eyes and didn't open them until she heard Crystal gasp. As soon as she did so, she almost fainted because she saw that they were almost fifty feet high up in the air. The chariot was in the air and they were flying.

'I told you, with me, you travel in style!' Welna called out. 'The ice giant will be following us. We better move fast.'

Sara looked around. They were flying right above the trees now and had almost reached the edge of the water body. Her head reeled as she took this all in.

The chariot itself was beautiful, decorated in white and blue. In the front, pulling it, were four beautiful pale white stallions with their manes tipped with black. They were so pale that they appeared ethereal, almost translucent, fading in and out of vision as the clouds drifted past them. The reins, in Welna's hands, were silver. As Sara stared at Welna's bare neck, once adorned by the necklace, she realized with a start that the chariot was exactly like the one she had seen on

Welna's necklace. The charm had come to life! She bent over the sides and looked out. The wheels were huge, with carved blue spokes. At one end of the chariot was a table that had all kinds of odds and ends lying on it—sheaves of papers, ink wells, pens, pencils, a magnifying glass, an old shield, a wooden spear and some gold beads, amongst others. Sara guessed that the table had been enchanted so that it, or the things on it, didn't topple off as the chariot flew.

Her train of thoughts was interrupted by a roar. This was followed by a crash. Sara saw the ice demon running through the trees, straight at them. He was tall and the chariot was almost exactly in line with the demon's nose.

Seeing him, all the weariness, tiredness and exhaustion of the day seemed to wash over the girls and a feeling of hopelessness threatened to take over. The giant roared and raised an icy hand, as if to pluck the chariot out of the sky.

'Hold on!' Welna shouted.

'To what?' Crystal asked, but she didn't get an answer as just then the chariot swung sharply to the left throwing both the girls to the side. 'Ow!' yelled Sara, clutching her shoulder. The manoeuvre was successful; the giant's hand missed the chariot by an inch.

He growled in anger and thrust his sword into the chariot. The girls moved away in the nick of the time.

'You think fire will help?' Sara shouted as Welna turned sharply. They had reached the water body but Welna had to swerve away from it and back into the forest to avoid getting crushed.

Jasmine swiped at the giant with her paw experimentally, as if to intimidate it.

'It might, I don't think that we are in any shape to summon the *power* of fire again!' Crystal replied.

'Listen I don't know what to do. But I'm guessing that will help!' Welna screamed at the top of her voice. Sweat beaded her forehead as she clutched the reins harder. She looked deathly pale and the girls noticed that the wound on her shoulder had reopened, drenching the fabric with blood.

'Hold on to something, will you?' Welna screamed as a ball of ice the size of a truck hurtled towards them. She cracked the reins and the horses dived forward, plunging the chariot into a free fall. The chunk of ice whooshed past.

'Stop it!' Sara screamed. She was scared of heights and the feeling of free falling was making her head spin.

Jasmine was thrown to the front of the chariot where she lay, crushed in one corner, struggling to get up. She growled a few times, disgusted at her own helpless state. Then she passed out.

'Just hold on for a few more minutes, Sara! You can do it!' Crystal assured her but Sara couldn't help screaming. This wasn't some ride in Disneyland! It was real life and if anything went wrong, which always did, people were gonna die.

'Let's just try and outrun it…it'll probably just melt in the sun!' Welna shouted. 'Like that's gonna happen,' Sara muttered sarcastically, her eyes shut tight, her head in one hand while she held on to Crystal with the other. 'Pull out of the dive! *Please.* Now!'

Another ball of ice came flying their way and this time they were not so lucky. Still not having pulled out of the dive, Welna wrenched the reins to one side just in time to alter their course to avoid the fatal collision. But they had misgauged the distance. The chunk grazed the side of a chariot, chipping off part of the wheel.

'No!' Crystal screamed as they spun out of control and headed towards the ground. Sara's nails dug painfully into Crystal's soft flesh. The giant roared triumphantly and banged his fist on the ground.

Round and round they spun, hurtling closer and closer to the ground. They fell through the ivory trees. The branches and leaves scratched the girls. The horses went mad in fear, tossing their heads and neighing, trying to get back control of the chariot.

They could see the giant running towards them as they fell. Now they were only a few feet from the ground. Now only ten …only five…

The ice giant extended his hand to crush them.

Sara couldn't stand it anymore. She opened her mouth and let out a terrifying scream that reverberated through the air. Crystal followed suit as she clung on to one side of the chariot and with the other hand held on to Sara who looked dangerously ill.

'This is the height of my bravery!' Sara cried and then added after an afterthought, 'Pun not intended.'

Crystal's heart was pounding so hard that it hurt. She only nodded.

'If I die now, I'm going to haunt the all of you for the rest of your lives!' Sara cried.

'What if we all die?' Welna asked, quite unnecessarily.

'Then I'm gonna make life miserable for the gods above and this ice demon below!' Sara shouted indignantly.

Now they were only two feet away from the ground…one…

Crystal closed her eyes, steeling herself for the crash. Sara dug her nails into Crytal's arms. Then at the last moment, with a humongous effort, Welna managed to pull the reins in just inches off the ground. The chariot swung dangerously to one side, scraped the ground and finally, shot upwards.

Crystal opened her eyes and heaved a sigh of relief. But as soon as the horses began to climb upwards and gain altitude Welna slumped to the floor, cradling her injured arm. The pulling in of the reins had cost her—her already wounded shoulder was twisted in the socket and was now dislocated.

Sara let go of Crystal's arm to move towards Welna. But the thrust of the chariot threw her backwards and she went tumbling out of the rear of the chariot.

'Sara!' Crystal screamed and Welna looked up horrified.

Jasmine, who was still passed out, oblivious of the surroundings, fortunately didn't fall off the chariot but lay to one side

For Sara it was a nightmare coming true as she hurtled out of the chariot. In every individual's life there is a time when they succumb to blind panic. That is when you flail and blindly do whatever you think will help. Then, when you figure that nothing is going to help, you succumb to wild panic. Such was the state of Sara's mind at this time.

As she fell, Sara flailed around for a hand hold desperately. Morbid thoughts of a hideous death squashed into a grease spot of arms and legs forced their way into her mind.

In that split second, her hand brushed against the metal edge of the chariot. She grabbed hold of it and hung there in mid-air, dangling between life and death. A line of dark blood traced a route down her palm all the way to her shoulder as the hard metal cut through her flesh.

Meanwhile, the ice giant was evidently not having a good time in the blazing heat. He stood up from his crouching position on the ground and grunted loudly. Whether he was melting or sweating profusely no one could tell. Big blobs of water fell from his forehead onto the trees. His fingers leaked water sporadically. He opened his gaping mouth and water squirted out of it, along with traces of floating dark liquid.

'Ew!' Sara managed to say as the stream of water barely missed her feet. 'Ice giant puke!'

Even though the giant was not in a perfect state, he still had enough in him to crush them into human pancakes.

The horses continued their ascent upwards but Sara's hands steadily grew bloodier.

'Hang on!' Crystal cried as she rushed to the side to offer an arm to Sara.

'As if I have a choice!' Sara murmured as she grasped Crystal's outstretched arm.

'Stop acting smart, I may just drop you!' Crystal said, grimacing from Sara's weight. 'Sara! You hand is bleeding!'

'Really? I never noticed!' Sara said sarcastically as Crystal clamped her arm over Sara's hand and tried to pull her up.

Welna struggled to get up and finally managed to scramble up to her feet. She gritted her teeth and held her dislocated arm. Beads of sweat appeared on her face as she slowly moved her shoulder. She gave a muffled shout of pain and as the shoulder popped back into the socket, her face twisted in a spasm of pain. She wiped her wet forehead with a trembling hand and after a helpless glance in Sara's direction, rushed to control the reins as the unguided horses where now going haywire.

Safe at last! thought Sara. It was a close one. Sara rested the very tips of her fingers on the steel edge as leverage and tightened her grip on Crystal's arm. Welna swerved the chariot to avoid a tree. A moment later, the ice giant barged out of the trees into view, water still streaming out of his mouth. A gasp of fear escaped Sara and she almost lost her grip on Crystal's hand, but her friend held on. She took a shaky breath and once again started to hoist herself up. All this blood loss was making her sick and the gashes on her palm grew deeper and throbbed.

She was still not fully on the chariot, her bloody hand slipped from Crystal's grasp and as her other hand was only resting by mere fingertips, she was sure that she would catapult down to certain death or die by the hands of the giant who was loping towards them like a great big ape.

At that very instant Crystal lunged forward and caught hold of Sara's palm.

'You two doing alright there?' Welna shouted out without turning. The horses where proving to be a challenge to control as they were thoroughly startled. The chariot, having lost a wheel, was still a bit wobbly.

Sara gasped as her hand slipped a little again and she slid a few inches down. Crystal nodded at her encouragingly and inch by inch started to hoist Sara up.

The demon was closing in. It roared and punched his fist in the direction of the girls. Immediately a gust of ice cold wind hit the chariot. Sara was lifted into the air and sent crashing inside the chariot. Welna fell flat on her rear but still managed to keep a grip on the reins. The horses whinnied and tossed their manes in nervous frustration as they galloped upwards. Crystal too was dashed against the carved sides of the chariot. She doubled over in pain as her shoulders hit the chariot. The ice giant was very close, close enough to grab the chariot as it crossed the jungle and flew over the water body—the colour of the water indicating that they were very near its middle.

As the chariot swerved once again, Sara flew across from one end to another and hit her head hard on something. She felt around and discovered a rounded corner and a polished surface. She deduced that she had crashed against the table full of odds and ends. From the corner of her eyes she noticed that the giant was very close now.

She looked around and saw that Crystal was bent over in pain and Welna was struggling to stand back up. On a sudden impulse, Sara groped around the table and her fingers closed around something like a wooden shaft. She dragged it to the corner and dropped it into her lap. It was a wooden spear.

The ice giant was closing in. In desperation, she picked up the spear and threw it at the giant with all her force. The blood on her palms had smeared the spear, giving it a reddish hue around its centre. She concentrated all her energies on the spear—all the anger, hurt and frustration and a fierce desire to live and save her mother that she had felt since she landed in Catriona. As she had hoped, the spear burst into flames in mid-air and landed right inside the demon's eye. It was a lucky throw since Sara knew she was not much of a shot. But as soon as the tip of the spear touched one of the pale blue eyes of the demon, it shattered into a million pieces, like shards of glass.

It had opened up a gaping hole, most probably the inside

of his empty head. The demon gave a scream and fell writhing to the ground.

'In the normal course of things, you should never have done that, because you're literally throwing away a weapon. But considering that these are not the most ideal of conditions, I must congratulate you on your presence of mind!' said Welna, still breathless.

Sara's shoulder was numb with pain and her throat was parched. Her stomach hurt like mad and as a fit of dizziness overcame her. Sara just had time to give Welna a wan smile and think, 'Why am I the only one who passes out again and again!' before red spots danced in front of her eyes and she passed out.

11

No sooner had she passed out, did she start dreaming.

She found herself in a dark cellar. It smelled of rotten vegetables and dead mice. A strange mist hung over the cellar, making it difficult for her to see clearly. She could make out that the sides of the cellar were stacked with barrels of wine. A faint light glowed in the corner of the room. Sara walked towards it. As she came closer she saw that the light was coming from two spheres that looked like diamonds. Thin, spidery threads emerged from these blue lights. They seemed so fragile and delicate that Sara instinctively held her breath as if her breathing could snap the thin threads. As she approached she noticed two figures on either sides of the sphere. The figures turned. For a second, Sara's heart stopped.

'M-M--Mom?' she whispered. 'And Aunt Vi!'

Olivia had always been 'Vi' and Anastasia 'Annie' to the children. The first figure smiled. 'Sara! Finally! We got through to you!' said Olivia.

'Where *are* we?' Sara asked, mystified.

'In the cellar of the palace, dear child,' Anastasia said. 'This is where Merissa keeps us to spin the Oracess.'

'The what?' asked Sara.

'The Oracess. It is the thread which keeps the magic in Catriona alive, but more importantly it strengthens and makes the queen's magic stronger than that of others,' said Olivia. 'This is the sphere or Oracess from which we spin the thread'.

As Sara examined the sphere closely she saw that the colours of the sphere kept changing depending on the angle from which she looked into the sphere, in the same way that you could see the colours of the rainbow when you turned a diamond in your hand.

Sara gritted her teeth. She couldn't bear the thought of her mother and aunt shut away in this ugly place while Merissa ruled above.

'The sphere. What's with the rainbow lights inside it?' Sara asked.

To her surprise, Vi and Annie shrugged their shoulders simultaneously.

'We don't really know. It's some kind of refraction of the light,' Vi said.

'Refraction of light's art always touches the heart!' Anastasia winked at Sara who smiled at her mother's sudden spurt of poetry.

'There is so much to tell you and so little time,' said Olivia suddenly serious. 'Do you know why only the four gems that make the Moon Wand are important?'

'What four gems?' asked Sara.

'We have been trying to talk to you since Peter informed

that he had finally succeeded in summoning both of you here. He told us all that had happened. Remember the piece of paper that Peter gave you when he had come to summon you here in the guise of that old man?' Vi asked. Sara nodded.

'The names of the gems written in that piece of paper are the gems that you need for the Moon Wand.'

Sara suddenly remembered that chit of paper that was still lying in their backpack with the names of four gems written on it. The old man had vanished after handing them that chit.

'Can you tell us why those are so important?' Anastasia pressed on.

'Are you going to ask all the questions and give me no answers, Mom? Vi?' Sara said, whining a little.

'Don't whine, Sara!' snapped Anastasia, suddenly unable to curb the motherly urge to chide. 'Be a sport and guess at least!'

'Um...because they are magic?' Sara answered hesitantly.

'But *why* are they magic?' questioned Anastasia.

Sara was silent.

'Because each of them contain a portion of the true queens' magic,' Olivia volunteered.

'And,' continued Anastasia. 'They also have our reflections etched into them.'

'The gems are very powerful and they have a lot of magical energy stored inside them. Every true queen who has reigned over Catriona, including us, has added a little of her life force into it to prepare a method of defeating any evil that might threaten the existence of Catriona, only to be used if the need for them ever arises. The reflections also change with every new reign. That's why the gems have our reflections etched in them because although Merissa rules the kingdom, we are the true queens of Catriona,' Olivia finished.

'And beware Sara, you will only have one chance to defeat Merissa. Once you use the Moon Wand, all its power will be unleashed all at once and all those centuries of hard magic will be spent in a split second. You and Crystal must decide when you want to use it. No one else can help you in this,' Anastasia warned ominously.

Silence cloaked the place as Sara took all this in.

'Mom, how can I defeat Loki?' Sara asked finally.

'With the Moon Wand, my child. The wand will also help you defeat Loki,' Anastasia said.

Suddenly they heard footsteps coming down the stairs.

'You must go now. Someone is coming this way. There will be trouble if they see you,' said Olivia. 'One last thing before you go,' she added. 'Always trust your necklaces. And Welna, trust her too. Tell Crystal I miss both of you but I am glad to know that you are in safe hands.'

'One last question,' asked Sara urgently. 'Why...why is Merissa keeping you alive? I mean, I'm glad that you are alive, of course...but she could spin the Oracess herself, couldn't she?'

Anastasia and Olivia smiled a sad smile. 'Because only the true queens of Catriona can spin the Oracess and keep the kingdom prosperous,' said Anastasia. 'Now go!'

Anastasia and Olivia stretched their hands outwards and a blue light pushed Sara backwards. She heard Olivia say, 'Goodbye! We'll miss you!'

'NO!' shouted Sara, waking up. 'Mom! Vi!' She was drenched in sweat. The smell of the cellar still lingered in her memory. 'Was it just a dream?' she wondered.

'Sup, dude!' said Crystal. 'I see you have woken up.'

'Where are we?' asked Sara, dazed. In a moment all the events of the day came rushing back to her.

'On Welna's flying chariot, of course,' said Crystal, looking surprised.

Sara stood up awkwardly. 'And the giant's still hot on our trail,' added Crystal, as Sara heard the faint growl of the giant in the distance.

∽

12

'Sara! Are you alright?' Welna turned around. She looked concerned.

'Yeah, but Welna, I had thi—' Sara started.

'Later!' Crystal shouted and dived away just as a chunk of ice came sailing at them and Welna steered the chariot into another dive.

'Again?' Sara asked as she clutched the table to keep her balance. Her head was still throbbing from hitting the table.

Crystal gave her a grim smile as she slid her bracelet out of her hand. She held it for a moment before it turned into her precious bow and a quiver of arrows appeared, slung over her shoulder.

'Find a way to defeat this big ape while I keep his tiny brain occupied. I honestly don't think I'll be able to last long, with magic or without,' Crystal said as she drew out a bow and let loose an arrow.

It flew through the air but had no impact on the giant.

It only bounced off the giant's chest. It did get his attention however. His one unharmed eye turned towards Crystal and he bared his humongous ice teeth.

Crystal drew three arrows from her quiver and shot them simultaneously inside the mouth of the demon. The fierce focus with which the arrows were shot had their impact. Midway to the giant, the arrows burst into flames and landed right inside the giant's mouth.

Almost immediately Crystal fell down to one knee with hardly any strength left.

'Crystal...!' Sara started forward but fell back when Crystal held up her hand and stopped her

'Go figure out a way to stop it. *Fast*!' She got to her feet and raised her bow again. Her face looked pale and sweat poured down her face.

As Crystal drew her bow, the diamond inlaid in it caught the sunlight and flashed in Welna's eyes as she turned around, dazzling her.

'Refraction!' she said, shielding her eyes. She then turned back and twisted the reins, urging her stallions to go faster, and the chariot turned and spun past the giant back into the jungle.

Sara thought fast: the ice demon could only be burnt with fire but they couldn't use magic because none of them had enough reserves left to create fire. So the only other option was to find a source of fire or build a fire manually. Building a fire would require several things—matchboxes and dry materials, for instance—and even if they had those things, how would they use it against the giant? No, they needed to find a source of heat. She looked around hastily but found nothing. Her heart sank. What if I used up my reserves to burn the giant? Then at least Crystal and Welna could go on, Sara thought, her mouth suddenly dry.

The sun beat down upon her and her skin was wet with sweat. It was very hot.

'Wait a second…heat!' She looked up and her eye caught the sun directly. She immediately looked away, her heart racing.

The sun could be their source of fire and heat. If she only knew how to harness its power …

She remembered something her mother has said, *'Refraction of light's art always touched the heart.'*

Sara suddenly ran towards the table and looked through its contents. Among various other objects was a magnifying glass.

Her heart thudding, Sara grabbed it, and ran to where Crystal stood. Crystal didn't look up. Her face was screwed up in concentration as she shot arrow after arrow at the demon. It didn't affect the giant, but it was so preoccupied with Crystal's arrows that he no longer shot balls of ice at them.

'Fast,' was the only thing that Crystal said to her.

Sara dropped down on the floor of the chariot and held the magnifying glass a little away from the floor.

After a little jiggling around, a thin beam of light appeared from the underside of the magnifying glass and fell on the floor. Immediately the floor started smoking a little. Hurriedly Sara refocused the magnifying glass in a way that she thought would focus the light on the giant. But it didn't happen. She tilted it a little backwards, away from the sun, and the beam of light moved from the floor and onto the giant's chest. The giant roared with pain but kept advancing on them.

Sara was frantic. This had to work! There was no way

they could survive otherwise. But the beam was very weak. Next to her, Crystal collapsed with exhaustion against the chariot floor. She grasped Sara's shirt and pulled her down.

'The heart…the heart…' Crystal whispered.

Sara felt desperate as she saw Crystal collapse. She focused the glass again and the beam flickered for a moment. It was still weak. She closed her eyes and concentrated, picturing the burning sun and the melting ice giant. She felt herself warm up as she imagined the vast energy reserve of the sun. She visualized a beam of light from it filling her up with energy and imagined the weak beam of heat from the magnifying glass becoming stronger.

As her eyes opened, she felt revitalized and to her happiness the beam of light now burned brighter and sharper. It had brought the giant to a standstill.

'Welna! Hold it! Don't move the chariot so much,' Sara said as the beam flickered momentarily.

Welna nodded. The giant roared. It was getting weaker and sweating gallons of water.

With a ferocious growl the demon beat his chest Tarzan style and started throwing ice chunks at them again. As they hurtled towards them, they all missed the chariot by a fraction of an inch or so. Without shifting the position of the magnifying glass in her hands, Sara turned slowly, thoroughly surprised. Welna stood in the same place but with her reins in one hand and the other hand outstretched. She smiled at Sara even though she looked exhausted.

With a start, Sara understood that Welna had used her mastery over the wind to deflect the ice. Even though she was only an amateur in the world of magic, Sara understood the amount of determination, energy and skill that was required to accomplish a task like that.

She gave Welna a thankful smile before concentrating on the beam again. She imagined the demon's heart beating away inside its slowly melting body, burning in the sun. Then suddenly, in a moment of morbid visualization, she pictured the demon's heart bursting and his body shattering into a thousand glittering pieces.

Her eyes flew open in horror. It seemed as though her world was collapsing around her. For a moment the hulking form of the ice giant loomed over the chariot and then, as if in slow motion, the giant shattered into shards of pointed ice. And amidst all the pieces was the heart, red and almost torn apart, but still recognizable. A strange substance oozed out of it which Sara realized was blood—the giant's heart *did* have blood in it then, she thought.

The blood fell to the ground with a resounding splatter and with a distinctive tinkle all those thousands of ice shards rained down on the chariot.

Sara heard Welna scream and was brought back to reality. Those shards could tear them apart. Welna had already exhausted much of her magical reserves and she was doing all that she could to keep the chariot airborne. And Crystal and Jasmine...

Thinking of them lying helpless and vulnerable brought back all her initial terror. Tossing the magnifying glass into the air, she did the most instinctive thing—she screamed.

All her terror and horror came flowing out of her in her voice.

The air around her shimmered and everything seemed to

become a little distorted.

A flash of light. Incredible pain. And then through the darkness she was falling...falling....

~

Sara blinked. Her head throbbed and red spots danced before her eyes. She blinked and looked up. She saw a clear blue sky tinged with the slightest red and a few stray patches of clouds.

She was sitting, no lying, sprawled on one side of the chariot with her head on its steel edge.

She sensed that someone was nearby and turned her head slowly. Pain erupted between her eyes and she winced. She turned and found Welna's violet eyes peering at her, an inch from her face.

'I'm fine! But what happened? Did I black out?' Sara asked, certain that she had blacked out for hours together.

'You didn't black out,' Welna said to her surprise. She then walked back to the front of the chariot and took the reins in her hands again. Her shoulder wound was still bleeding but it seemed to have healed a little.

'Here, have these,' she threw something towards Sara. It was white and slightly sticky. It looked like a square piece of...

'Is this chocolate?' Sara asked, surprised.

'Smart girl! Yes, it is. Eat it, it'll make you feel better,' Welna said.

'Can I have a dark chocolate? I hate whites,' said Sara eyeing the square disappointedly. Welna sighed and snapped her fingers. The square of white changed to dark chocolate.

'Crystal! Jasmine!' Sara suddenly cried and staggered towards them. Jasmine was still lying unharmed under the table but Crystal was moaning and had high fever.

'Has she fainted? Will she be alright?'

'Yes and no. She's just exhausted. Give her some chocolate too,' Welna replied.

Sara gently put Crystal's head on her lap. She broke the chocolate in two and forced some chocolate into Crystal's mouth as she nibbled on her half of the chocolate.

'So…what happened?' Sara asked revelling in the warmth that was spreading through her body.

'You let your imagination run wild,' Welna leaned on the chariot so that she could face Sara and still control the reins. 'And we have almost crossed the water body.'

Sara looked over the side. They were indeed nearing the other bank.

'I know that part. I imagined it and it came true, although it was pretty gruesome,' Sara shuddered at the memory of the raw heart.

Welna nodded knowingly. 'Yeah, but then you screamed,' she said simply.

'I screamed,' Sara nodded. 'Then what?'

'I don't know if you meant to do it or it was by mistake; but all your emotions got channeled through that single scream in such a way that it created a kind of force field that deflected all the ice pieces. But the blast was huge and you were thrown sideways and hit your head on the edge of the chariot. All this happened in a split second and I spurred the horses right then and they took us away from that spot. You didn't black out, but it was a few moments before your mind focused again and you were able to open your eyes,' Welna explained with an approving smile. 'But you are exhausted because of the day's events and your head is hurting because you injured it, not because of the magic you used. You didn't use your own reserves to create the force field, so your magical reserves were not depleted. This is actually how you do good magic, by finding different ways to channel your magical powers with minimal loss of energy.'

Sara inhaled sharply. She still couldn't believe that she had done this. She promised herself that she would control her imagination from now on.

'Is that chocolate?' Crystal tried to sit upright but fell back immediately.

'Not so fast, sis! Chill…the demon's gone and you did a great job,' Sara said laughing and stroking Crystal's hair.

'Jasmine,' Welna said to the pair who had momentarily forgotten the dog. 'She'll be alright too. I checked on her. She's just sleeping now. She regained consciousness halfway through the…let's say 'battle' for want of a better word… and would have been prepared to charge right back inspite of her exhaustion. So I put a sleeping spell on her,' Welna said, almost guiltily.

'It was the right thing to do,' Crystal said amused. 'What happened while I was out?'

Welna and Sara exchanged glances and then recounted what had happened.

'A force field? That is so cool! You've *got* to teach it to me some day!' Crystal said.

'No! It's not amazing! Don't you see? I messed it up! All of you could have died because of my stupid imagination!' Sara said covering her face with her hands.

'Hey—hey, it's alright! We're still here, right? And it's

thanks to you that the giant's gone and we're alive!' Crystal said sitting up and putting her arm awkwardly around Sara.

Sara looked up and smiled through her watery eyes.

'Are you crying?' asked Crystal knowing what Sara's retort would be. She was trying to provoke Sara into a mock fight. She winked at Welna who stood watching her two nieces, amused.

'No I'm not!' Sara said indignantly, quickly brushing away a tear when she thought no one was seeing.

A stifled laugh escaped Welna.

'What?' asked Sara, angrily.

Welna shook her head and turned away.

'Yes you were!' Crystal said, laughing.

'Of course not!' said Sara. She was laughing too now.

'You should really see yourself cry! It's so funny!' Crystal said. 'Remember the tree house incident?'

Sara turned faintly pink before answering. 'There was a dead insect in my shoe! And I stepped on it in my socks!'

Welna burst out laughing.

'What about that time at that club, Crystal? Boo-hoo! I want to stay for some more time!' Sara mimicked.

'I was thirteen, for God's sake!' Crystal was appalled that Sara remembered that.

~

For half an hour they flew over serene surroundings, pleasantly bickering among themselves. It was already dark when Welna finally announced 'We're here.' She reined in the air horses and they instantly dipped forward, landing smoothly.

The girls climbed down. In front of them was a small

but beautiful clearing, bathed in moonlight.

'Wow!' said Crystal admiringly while Sara ran into the clearing.

'This rocks!' cried Sara and ran into the clearing followed by Crystal and then Welna who walked slowly.

'Why are we here?' Sara asked as Welna walked up to them.

'This is where we'll rest for today,' Welna replied.

'But where's the VOO?' asked Crystal.

'"VOO?"' asked Sara confused.

'"Valley of Ordnance."' Crystal said impatiently before turning to Welna.

'Between the mountains and the Water Body there is this narrow stretch of forested area,' Welna explained. 'This clearing is in the middle of the forested area. Tomorrow we will travel to Valley of Ordnance. It will hardly take us an hour to get there.'

'Good news!' said Sara. 'Now for some food.'

'Oh yes! Food!' said Welna. To the girls' utter amazement, Welna waved her hands and an entire feast appeared before them laid out on a fresh white cloth.

'Amazing!' shouted Crystal and dashed to the food. Sara followed.

'Woof!' a joyous bark greeted them. She turned quickly to see Jasmine sitting on Welna's lap. 'I see someone has woken up! You were amazing, Jasmine!' Sara said ruffling Jasmine's fur affectionately.

'Now let's eat,' said Sara. She plonked herself down and was going to help herself when Welna stopped her.

'I am the wind princess and you are the princesses of

Catriona, you will not eat this way. Now look at me,' Welna said. She sat down and made herself comfortable. Then she raised her hand. 'Plate! Some ham and bacon sandwiches, the tomatoes and a glass of the milk,' she ordered. Before their eyes, invisible hands plated up the things that Welna had asked for and politely handed the plate to her. Welna looked at her nieces. 'Go ahead!' she said encouragingly.

'Um...plate! Bring me some sandwiches, a piece of roast turkey, the herb potatoes and a glass of creamy milk,' Sara said uncertainly. The plate filled itself up and flew to Sara. She grabbed it before it could fall. 'Wow!' she murmured to herself.

Crystal tried next. She was a lot more confident. 'Plate! Bring me some fresh tomatoes, some cheese, some chicken and a glass of milk,' she said. The plate flew to Crystal. She accepted it and started eating. 'It's delicious!' she said taking a bite.

'You know, we didn't have to cross the Water body through Merlandia after all,' Crystal mused.

Sara nodded her mouth too full of food to answer.

After they had all eaten their fill, Welna snapped her fingers and everything disappeared. Then they lay down on their backs and looked up at the stars. Sara thought about everything that had happened. She thought about her mother and aunt, shut away in some dark, musty cellar while Merissa ruled the kingdom. They had to make the Moon Wand and defeat Merissa.

She had to tell Crystal and Welna about her dream. She sat up intending to tell them but both of them were already fast asleep. Her own arms and legs hurt. She lay down and before long she fell asleep as well.

13

'Get up, people! Time to go!' Welna shouted. It was one of those pleasant days when the warmth of the sun was undercut by a gentle breeze to make sure you didn't feel hot.

'Huh?' Sara sat up groggily and rubbed her eyes. 'Morning already?' she asked.

'Crystal! Crystal, wake up!' shouted Welna.

But Crystal just snored away. 'CRYSTAL!' yelled Welna into her ear. 'Huh! Monster! Where? Where?' Crystal woke up with a start, looking around, ready to fight.

Sara giggled.

'No monsters, but we need to get going!' Welna laughed.

'Oh, okay,' Crystal said blushing. 'Stop laughing, Sara!'

Jasmine barked and gave Crystal a big lick. Crystal patted her fondly.

'Let's get going!' Welna said cheerfully. 'We have to reach the Valley today.'

'I wonder what awaits us there,' Sara said.

They had a simple breakfast of eggs, bacon and milk and set off. After walking for what seemed like ages, they pushed through a curtain of creepers and emerged out of the forest.

'Oh my gosh!' cried Crystal.

'Wow!' Sara gasped.

'Woof!' Jasmine barked in approval.

Up ahead was a lush field full of flowers and trees. Beyond that, on either side of the field, stretched a range of snow-capped mountains as far as the eye could see. The sight was breathtaking. 'The silver mountain glints because of the countless silver armours that are lying around there. Those armours make a person really powerful. The person has to climb up there and fulfil a quest from the owner of the silver armour. If he comes back alive he gets the armour,' Welna explained. 'And that is the Mashinalavae Hill,' she added, pointing.

'But why do they call the valley between these two the Valley of Ordnance?' asked Crystal.

'That's because the people in the Valley make weapons but if you want a weapon then you go on a quest. If you come back alive you get the weapon. But the quests are deadly! Believe me, this is the last place you would like to take up a quest,' said Welna.

The valley in front of them was unusually large. It was grassy and beautiful, but strangely enough, there were no people around, and no place that looked like it was hiding a celestial Aquamarine gem. They all looked at each other in confusion.

'I have never been here before, so I don't know a thing about this place. Anyway, let's eat. It's almost lunch time.' Once again Welna snapped her fingers and a feast appeared. They ate in silence thinking about their next move.

'Guys,' Sara started. 'When I had blacked out on the chariot, I had a dream. I saw Mom and Vi, your mom, Crystal, in that dream.'

Crystal sat up. 'My mom and Annie?'

'Yeah, and they spoke to me,' said Sara and then she told them all about her dream. After she finished she looked at Welna. Her face was serious. 'Sara, what you experienced was your soul travelling to your mother. The queens summoned you there. That kind of magic takes a lot of power and is used only when something really important has to be told or explained,' Welna said gravely.

'Okay,' said Sara. 'But why me? Why not Crystal?'

'Maybe because they can only contact one of you at a time. They might have tried to contact both of you and maybe they got to you first,' said Welna.

'Oh,' was all Sara could say. 'We better get going. We have to find the people of the Valley.'

They started walking towards the valley, keeping a keen eye out for any sign of civilization.

As they entered the valley it hit them...right on the face. What hit them was how pleasant the place was. A little too pleasant maybe, thought Sara, ominously. It looked even prettier than when they had seen it from afar. The beauty of the valley was only marred by a cave with lighted lamps at the entrance. The lamps were lit even in the daylight.

A warm draught of air hit them as they entered the meadow, making them feel warm and cosy. A yummy smell of freshly baked bread and cake wafted through the whole place. 'What's happening?' she asked groggily. Every moment of tiredness they had ever experienced in their life seemed to come back to them. The only aim in life that seemed worth while right then was to just stretch out on the meadow and sleep...forever. Welna yawned. Jasmine whined and curled up, ready to sleep.

'We...should...not...sleep,' Welna said before dropping to the ground. Sara and Crystal stretched out beside her.

'It...maybe...a trap,' Sara said, yawning.

'Let's...sleep...no...harm,' Crystal mumbled before she started snoring. After a moment, Sara dropped down gently on the grass and fell fast asleep.

~

Crystal woke up to see the sun shining overhead. Her hands felt like they had been tied to the ground. In an instant, she realized that they *were* tied to the ground! She turned her head and saw that her hands, feet, clothes and even her hair were pinned to the ground with thousands of ropes and tiny pins each the size of a thumb nail. She tried moving her hands, but the pins and the ropes were amazingly strong. She felt something crawl on to her legs. She wasn't scared of insects, but she found them gross, especially if they crawled into her clothes. She looked down and saw hundreds, no thousands, of finger-sized insects at her foot. Okay, that is getting weird, even by Catriona standards, she thought. Then one insect crawled on to her leg and made its way up to her chest.

'Please let it be a nice cute one, and not an ugly, gross one,' she prayed silently. Crystal opened her eyes and screamed— The insect jumped, and scurried back down. It was not an insect but a tiny man!

'What in the world...?' began Sara. She and Welna had been awakened by Crystal's scream. Crystal was still staring at the tiny people.

'Oh my God!' cried Sara. 'What *are* they?'

'Um...Sara, I think you mean *who* are they,' Welna said, eyeing them suspiciously.

Sara looked at them carefully and stifled a scream. 'No way in my whole life is this possible!' Sara said shaking her head in disbelief. 'It's right out of *Gulliver's Travels*, but in Catriona!'

'Woof! Woof!' Jasmine barked. She was tossing around trying to get out of the ropes that held her in place. The people who were advancing towards Jasmine backed away in fright.

Realizing that the girls were scared of them, one of the men boldly marched up Sara's legs and stopped at the base of her neck. He was about eight inches tall and wore a military uniform with many shining medals pinned on to it. Sara guessed that he was a commander of some sort.

'Uslecious amha harlaful?' he asked in voice that was barely audible.

'Huh?' asked Sara. Her voice was too loud for the tiny man. He instantly covered his ears.

'Oh, sorry,' she whispered. The officer looked surprised, maybe because he didn't expect an apology from a creature so big.

'Uslecious amha harlaful?' he asked again.

'Huh?' Sara whispered. 'I don't know what you're saying.'

'Who are you?' asked the officer.

'Um...we are the daughters of your true queens, Anastasia

and Olivia. This is our aunt Welna,' Sara introduced herself and everyone else.

Everyone had begun to murmur amongst themselves. Sara caught snatches of their conversations which sounded something like, 'Isfia craziny? Mallo madgess!' She couldn't make any sense of them but she had a feeling they weren't compliments.

Suddenly a boy ran up to her chest. She could tell that he was a small boy because he was even shorter than the men and had a girly face, bereft of any traces of facial hair.

He asked in a soft voice, 'El spegano nutos?'

When Sara looked at him confused he repeated in English, 'Are you nuts?' Sara stared at him incredulously. The crowd began to laugh.

'Listen, I have proof that I *am* the queen's daughter. Just free my hands and I'll show you,' Sara tried to move her arms. A thousand soldiers charged at her poking her with swords that pricked her. It was uncomfortable and it did hurt a little.

'Okay, okay!' her voice rose in annoyance but when the officer covered his ears, she continued in a lower voice. 'Look at my necklace.'

The officer leaned in to see itnearly tumbling down Sara's neck. He gasped and turned. Addressing the crowd he said, 'El spegano haso necklaces! You'll cano pullt hernow testila.' A murmur of approval ran through the crowd.

The officer once more turned to Sara. 'As you claim to be the daughter of the queens, then we shall now test you and see whether you are telling the truth or not,' he said in English. 'And make sure that dog doesn't bite,' he added.

Sara nodded. 'Jasmine, it's okay, girl, calm down.' Jasmine

looked at her for a moment and then settled down.

A man dressed in dirty clothes stepped forward.

'I am a farmer...' he began but sensing that she couldn't hear him, he scurried up her chest. 'I am a farmer,' he continued. 'And whenever the queens came to visit us, they would create more crops for us using magic...can you do that?'

Sara replied unhesitatingly, 'I am not sure I can, but Crystal can do it.'

'Um...Sara...I am not too sure about this,' Crystal answered, a bit worried.

'Relax! You can do it!' Sara replied winking.

'Mom, please help me!' Crystal muttered under her breath. 'But for doing this,' she added, 'You'll have to release me from these ropes.'

The officer standing on Sara jumped down and consulted a few others. 'Okay! But you dare not try any stunts,' the officer screamed to make himself be heard. He then motioned for a few soldiers to cut the ropes. They rushed to Crystal and sliced the ropes with their swords.

'Um...my hair too please,' Crystal told a soldier who was near her. They had forgotten to cut the ropes that were holding her hair. After the soldiers had cut the ropes holding her hair, Crystal stood up. She shook out her tangled black hair. The crowd gasped.

'She lookoso somano licese herow momeresa!' somebody remarked and Crystal was sure it meant, 'She looks so much like her mother.'

'You want plants, farmer?' she asked. 'Show me where you want them.'

'Over there!' he shouted. He pointed to a plot beside a

small hut. The house was surrounded by wilting flowers. 'What kind of grain do you want to grow?' Crystal asked.

'Um…wheat. Wheat, corn and barley,' the farmer replied.

Crystal held out her hands and closed her eyes. She closed her eyes and concentrated hard, imagining the house surrounded by her favourite flowers—reddish pink euphorbia. The house began to glow. The wilting flowers transformed themselves into euphorbia plants, bursting with flowers. A collective gasp rose from the crowd, but Crystal was not done yet. She channeled all her energy on to the plot of land. She imagined the field filled with wheat, corn and barley. She saw them swaying in the breeze, growing rapidly until they were ready to be harvested. A beautiful vivid green sphere formed in Crystal's outstretched hands. Out shot a single beam of light.

As the beam neared the plot of land, it branched out several beams and hit the earth. A moment later wheat, corn and barley started growing in different parts of the field. They grew and grew till they ripened and were ready to be harvested. Finally the light died down and Crystal opened her eyes. She saw what she had done and even though she was surprised at her powers she kept a straight face. But under that mask, she was ready to fall back down. She didn't know how she had done what she did; perhaps it was a dormant instinct that had been awakened but she wasn't sure that she would be able to do it again.

'Now are you convinced that I am Queen Olivia's daughter and Queen Anastasia's niece?' she demanded. No one answered. Sara and Welna too were gaping at her. Crystal took a step forward but staggered, tired by her magic, and steadied herself against a tree. Suddenly the little officer who had climbed on Sara shouted, 'All hail Princess Crystal of Catriona!' The crowd followed suit and soon everyone was hailing Crystal.

'Stop! Please stop!' Crystal said. 'I would like you to call me just Crystal. Please, no princess!' The crowd looked surprised but Welna understood that they were impressed by her humility. The officers turned to Sara. 'Now you!' he said. 'Prove yourself.'

A frail, old woman stepped forward. The officers helped her to Sara's chest. She spoke in a raspy voice. 'Can you see that parched bit of land over there?' When Sara nodded, the old woman went on, 'I live there with my grandson. I have a small plot of land. Every year we manage to make ends meet but for the past year there have been no rains. We have no crops and no money. I have taken money from almost everyone in this village and I want to pay them back. Can you please make it rain on my plot?'

Sara looked at the hut. It was missing a door and was almost falling apart.

'Please cut my ropes,' Sara said to the soldiers.

They cut her ropes and she stood up. She straightened her clothes and shook her hair out, like Crystal. Her brown hair glinted gold in the setting sun. She gathered her luscious hair and casually put it over one shoulder. 'Just one question, Grandma,' Sara said. 'Do you work in the field?' The old woman nodded. 'My grandson is too young to work,' she replied, tears glistening in her eyes.

'Don't worry, Grandma, your plot will be watered,' Sara said and walked a little way.

Then she closed her eyes and concentrated. She remembered

how she had channelled her emotions when she had accidently created that force-field and tried to do the same here. She thought of how unfair it was that the grandmother, so frail and elderly a woman, was still working. She summoned the power of the wind and storm. She concentrated for so long that the villagers started getting worried. Then her eyes flew open. Her eyes were now grey, rimmed with black.

Welna and Crystal gasped, they had never seen anything like that before. Sara closed her fists, and opened them. Her hair began flying in the wind. Thick black clouds gathered above the plot. It started to rain. But the rain was controlled, raining only on the old woman's field. Her magic was so powerful that the winds wrapped around her, gently levitated her. The rain made the parched earth wet again, but Sara realized that they were still not fertile. After a few minutes, Sara gently dropped to earth. The rains stopped. The storm clouds dispersed and her eyes returned to their normal colour. She concentrated on the soil. It turned a deep, rich black in front of the watching crowd. Sara blinked. She was not done. Her eyes turned towards the house. She imagined it whole again. She imagined it bigger, with all comforts that would make the life of the old lady simpler. She fixed her eyes on the house and held out her hands.

'How is she doing that?' asked Crystal, wonderstruck.

'Anastasia,' Welna whispered.

'What?'

'Anastasia! She's inherited it from Anastasia!' Welna said, awestruck. 'Anastasia's eyes always mirrored the colour of the element that she used to perform magic.'

'English,' said Crystal annoyed. 'Talk English!'

'Means if Anastasia used fire, her eyes turned amber, if she used wind, then steel grey,' Welna said impatiently. 'Now stop talking and watch!'

At first, nothing happened. Then the house was engulfed in an opaque purple sphere. No one could tell what was going on inside the sphere. A few moments later the sphere faded. The house was mended and freshly painted. Sara turned and smiled and took a shaky breath. The weight of the magic had completely drained her. She had a slight headache but she managed to keep her composure in front of the crowd.

'Have I proved myself enough?' she asked, smiling. 'Grandma, is there anything else I can do for you?' The old lady burst into tears. Sara picked her up.

'Don't cry, Grandma! A granddaughter can't bear to see her grandmother cry!'

The old woman wiped her tears. 'Thank you, my daughter!' she said. 'Do dine with us some day.' Sara smiled and nodded. She put the tiny old woman down and looked at the people. A thunderous applause broke out. Sara did a little curtsy.

'All hail Princess Sara, daughter of Queen Anastasia and niece of Queen Olivia!' the officer hailed.

'Princess Sara, huh? Has a nice ring to it, doesn't it?' she smiled, winking at Welna. 'But somehow it doesn't really suit me. Call me Sara!' she smiled at the little people.

'*She* still has to prove herself!' said an officer from the back, pointing at Welna.

'I am the *wind*!' Welna said.

'Prove yourself,' demanded the officer, adamant.

'This could get rough, do you still want it?' Welna asked smiling.

'Yes!' the officer replied.

'Fine! All children, the elderly and the weak, please step aside,' she said. The people did as they were told. When only the sturdy youths and officers were left, Welna grinned. She opened her fist and closed it. Immediately the people writhed in pain and fell to the ground. 'Enough proof?' asked Welna. The people, unable to speak, nodded their head. Welna opened her hand and the people fell down in exhaustion, gasping. After a moment, Sara and Crystal understood what Welna had done—she had pulled out the air from the area, leaving the people unable to breathe. Of course, after that display, the villagers hailed Welna too.

Crystal suddenly sensed a movement at her feet. She looked down and found the bold officer who had climbed on Sara. He was flanked on both sides by two other officers. They motioned for the three girls to bend down. Sara bent down and scooped all three of them into her palm. She held them close to her face. Crystal and Welna crowded beside her. The officer on the right cleared his voice. Sara suppressed a smile; the officer's throat clearing sounded like mouse's squeak.

'This officer,' he screamed to be heard, 'has committed the offence of imprisoning the princesses in ropes. Now his life is in your hands and you are free to punish him in any way.'

Sara's expression on hearing this must have been quite funny because Welna and Crystal burst out laughing.

'You...what exactly do you want us to do?' asked Sara.

'Depends on you!' said the officer, offended.

'We-well in that case, I have something to give him,' Welna said, trying to stop laughing. She leaned and whispered something to Crystal, who passed on the message to Sara.

Crystal made a horrible face. 'You dare to bind us with your filthy ropes?' she thundered. 'Now you shall face the consequences!'

The crowd below grew deadly silent. They waited with bated breath wondering what the punishment for the officer would be.

'But pri- princess, I was just ensuring the safety of this village,' the officer replied, quaking with fear.

'Exactly! You were ensuring the safety of this village so what you deserve is special!' Crystal replied.

'What you deserve is a...PROMOTION!' All three of them shouted out the last word together.

The officer nearly passed out in fright. The men escorting him looked confused.

'He did bind us, but he bound us to ensure the safety of your village. If we had not come in peace, and if—oh, your name is Larris?—and if Larris had not bound us, the village would not have survived! Thus, he deserves a promotion,' explained Sara.

'Please untie his chains.' Larris's chains were cut and he bowed in reverence.

'Now let's have some dinner.' Welna said, cheerfully. 'And,' she turned to the people, 'all of you are invited to dine with us.'

Welna snapped her hands and a giant table appeared set with plates, spoons and glasses. The only thing missing was food and drinks. The people looked at her curiously. Welna laughed. 'This is a magical spread,' she said. 'Just grab a plate, imagine what you wish to have and then it will appear on the plate.' There were three large plates and several smaller plates and glasses for the tiny people. The villagers scurried around gathering plates and helping themselves to whatever they wanted to eat and drink.

∽

14

Over dinner they talked. The girls came to know that the name of the village was Cilicia. Their king Akataria was imprisoned by Merissa because this was the only kingdom that refused to submit to her will.

The villagers also told the three girls that though they were small, they made excellent weapons. But they were gradually losing the metals they used to make weapons—Golden Sundust, Moonbeam Silver and Glazed Bronze. All these metals were extremely rare and not likely to be found anywhere else. Golden Sundust was a metal found deep inside the earth. According to the Cilicians, the soil of the land absorbed the rays of the sun and transformed them into a fine dust underground. This process took place deep inside the earth and therefore, Golden Sundust was very rare. Large amounts of Golden Sundust were required to make a single weapon.

Moonbeam Silver, the Cilicians continued, was specially imported from the Midnight Moonbeams Hill to make weapons. Thousands of moonbeams were tightly packed together to form a hard brick-like object that was melted in a forge and moulded to make weapons. However, only Midnight Moonbeam Hill could supply them with these moonbeams. The bricks of moonbeam took months to form, and thus this metal too was extremely rare.

Glazed Bronze, on the other hand, required mining and was found only in certain parts of Cilicia. Centuries ago, as the story went, the Norse goddess Idunn took pity on the Cilicians and presented them with a basket of golden apples to bury in Cilicia. Idunn's golden apples were famed because they bestowed eternal youth. Whenever a white streak of hair appears on the hair of the gods, they took a bit of a golden apple and the ageing would reverse. Idunn was therefore considered very auspicious in Norse mythology.

'So what do these apples do anyway?' interrupted Crystal.

'I am getting to that, and questions later please,' an old Cilician who had started the story replied politely. 'Idunn had told them that the apples would bring fertility and luck to the land and as long as the apples remained buried, the valley would never face a shortage of metals. These apples would help in speeding up the metal-forming processes. They would also absorb more sunlight, form the bricks quicker and bring the glazed bronze closer to the surface.

'But the weapons we made with these were given to only a chosen few, like the kingdom's army and the royals. Others who wanted them had to go on a quest. Till now, no one has ever returned alive from a quest. Then when Merissa came along, she wanted us to produce weapons for her, and we refused.'

'That is why our king was imprisoned,' another Cilician took up the story. 'But the Dark Creature that lives in that cave there,' he said, pointing at the cave, 'He works for Merissa. He stole our apples and buried them in his own garden. He now makes weapons for Merissa and her army. And believe me, he gets rewarded plenty. Now we can't make any weapons and if Catriona is to fight against Merissa, we need good weapons.'

'But things took a turn for the worse when Idunn was captured. It was on Merissa's orders. The Dark Creature was asked to kidnap Idunn along with her basket of apples. Merissa should *never* get her hands on the apples because if she gets hold of them, then she will remain young forever! And that would be disastrous for our kingdom!' On that ominous note, the Cilician ended his tale.

There was a silence as each of the girls considered the horrors that would be inflicted on the Catrionians if Merissa got hold of the apples.

'By the way, did you have any specific reason to come here?' Larris asked, breaking the silence.

Welna, Crystal and Sara looked at each other. 'This might sound a bit wacko but it is the truth…' began Sara. 'But we are actually trying to make the 'Moon Wand' to battle Merissa.'

The Cilicians stared at them for a moment. Then, the whole village erupted in a thunderous applause.

'By all means we shall help!' shouted someone.

'We have come here in search of the Aquamarine gem,' said Crystal. 'Can you show us where it is and how can we get it?'

The villagers drew in their breath.

'What? Did I say something wrong?' Crystal asked,

surprised. No one answered. They looked at each other.

'Please let this be an easy one! Please no fighting monsters or anything else!' Sara prayed to herself.

'All right,' said Larris finally. 'We will give you the gem.'

Sara blinked. 'Huh? No fighting monsters, no stealing anything, no nothing?'

'But,' Larris continued, 'As per tradition you have to take up a quest.'

Sara snorted. 'Of course! What was I thinking?'

'Why did you just snort like a full sized, fully fed, really angry bull?' asked Crystal, hearing her snort.

'I was just thinking about how my definition of easy totally changed since we started on this adventure!'

Crystal smiled. 'We'll make it, don't worry!' she said.

'Fine. But what is this quest?' asked Welna, coming straight to the point.

The Cilicians look at each other nervously. 'Your quest is to defeat the creature in the cave and get back our apples and Idunn,' an officer said.

'Huh? That's it?' Crystal asked.

'He's not small like us, he is bigger than you,' the officer warned.

'Sorry, your majesties, but we are bound to our tradition,' another officer said, bowing low.

Larris got up. 'May I have permission to go with the princesses?' he asked the people.

Sara would have very much liked that but judging by the looks on the people's faces they didn't seem very keen on the idea.

'Thanks Larris, but we don't want you to endanger your

life for us,' Sara replied smiling.

'You're right. We are the ones who have to do this!' Crystal said.

'Let's all get some sleep now. Tomorrow we shall get your apples and the goddess back,' Sara said.

'Jasmine, get up!' she gently nudged Jasmine who was sleeping on the grass beside her with her finger and woke her up. Jasmine got up, walked a few feet and stood staring at the moon.

The Cilicians then trooped back to their houses while the girls sat together to discuss their plan for the morning.

'You know, Jasmine has grown. It's hardly been a few days but she's almost twice her normal size. I wonder how you held her, Welna,' Sara said suddenly.

'She has grown because animals grow much faster in Catriona and they also live longer. And I also think that it's because of Skadi's blessings,' Welna explained. Sure enough, Jasmine looked twice as big as when they had started out. She looked beautiful as she stood there, the full moon behind her and her tail swaying gently. 'Come here, my big girl!' called out Sara, fondly. Jasmine bounded up and sat down heavily on her foot.

The girls then said good night and settled down to rest. The gentle breeze lulled the girls into a peaceful sleep. Tomorrow, they knew, was going to be an eventful day.

~

'Woof!' barked Jasmine into Sara's ear.

'Huh!' Sara was jolted awake. 'Oh it's you, Jasmine. You scared me.'

'Morning already?' asked Crystal stretching herself. 'Where's Aunt 'Wind'?'

'Here I am, and I told you not to call me Aunt!' Welna said appearing before them. She handed them each a bowl of cereal. 'Energy food!' she said cheerfully.

'Wow!" Crystal said to Sara. 'I wish *I* could be that happy about dying.'

Sara grinned.

'I heard that!' shouted Welna. She was giving Jasmine a little water and some food and humming to herself.

'Why is the wind princess in such high spirits?' Sara asked sitting cross-legged on the grass.

'I've figured something out!' Welna said.

'What's that?' asked Crystal, amused.

'Once we find Idunn, I figured out a way to get her back!" Welna said.

Sara and Crystal sat up.

'And how is that?' asked Sara.

'We turn her into a nut! Simple!' Welna said as if it were something as simple as brushing your hair.

'This is crazy. I thought you just said that we turn her into a nut! That's ridiculous!' Sara laughed.

'I said exactly what you thought I said,' Welna said, smiling. Sara just stared at her.

'But what if she's already a nut? You know, cuckoo in the head?' asked Crystal, twirling her finger in a circular motion near her temple.

'Yeah! I still have to meet a Norse god that I actually like,' Sara said shrugging.

"That was supposed to be a joke! You were supposed to

laugh!" Crystal raised her eyebrows in mock frustration.

"Oh, hahaha! Happy?" Sara said sarcastically.

"Drop it!" Welna said to Crystal who was ready with a retort. 'In the Norse myth,' Welna said, ignoring their jokes, 'When Idunn was kidnapped by—I forget who—when Idunn got kidnapped, Loki turned her into a nut and—.'

Crystal giggled.

'What is it?' asked Welna, exasperated.

'Nothing. It's just that—turned her into a *nut*—is funny,' she said, stifling a laugh.

Welna rolled her eyes. 'Anyway, Loki turned her into a nut,' She repeated, pointedly looking at Crystal. 'He turned himself into a falcon and flew to the other gods with Idunn as a nut in his claws,' Welna finished triumphantly.

'I still don't see what it has to do with us. We can't turn into birds! Nor can we turn her into a nut!' Crystal pointed out.

'You can't turn into birds but you *can* turn her into a nut! Crystal, your mother's speciality was the ability to turn stuff into something else. You'll have to be the one to turn her into a nut! You're the only one who can do it while I, Sara and Jasmine will keep whatever is there in that cave distracted,' Welna said earnestly.

'That's nonsense!' Crystal said starting to get annoyed. 'I have no clue how to do that!'

'You don't need to know how to do this! It's already there in you. Now listen, we go in, get Idunn and the apples and get out before we even see her captor, okay?'

'Sure, but who *is* Idunn's captor?' Sara asked. She had a feeling that she knew who the captor was but couldn't remember his name.

'I don't know! But I feel like I should!' Welna said.

Suddenly the sound of trumpets, though very faint, filled the air. Sara looked down and saw the Cilicians marching towards them.

'Time for the quest,' said Crystal, more cheerfully than she actually felt.

'Ready for your quest, your majesties?' Larris asked.

The girls looked at one another and said, 'Yes!' Welna looked at Crystal, surprised at the excitement with which she replied.

'Let's go and get killed!' said Crystal, sarcastic as always. 'Idunn, here we come!' yelled Sara.

Welna looked at both of them, bemused.

The old lady whose house Sara had mended staggered up to them. Crystal lifted her up. The other two crowded behind her.

'My darlings,' she said in a raspy voice. 'Listen to me carefully. I know where the goddess is imprisoned and kept, but I am forbidden from telling anyone directly. But what I can tell you is that her prison is guarded with modern and authentic enchantments, so be careful. And Idunn leaves golden traces.'

'Huh?' asked Crystal.

'Please, Grandma, can you explain this a little more clearly?' asked Welna.

'Daughter, I can't tell you more than this,' the old woman sighed.

Jasmine was curiously sniffing the villagers who were struggling to shoo her away. 'It's okay, she won't bite,' said Crystal laughing. 'Jasmine, come here.' Jasmine obediently trotted to Crystal's side. The villagers heaved a collective sigh of relief.

They led the girls to the edge of the village. 'We can only accompany you here till here,' Larris said.

'Uh-huh, thanks guys. We'll manage,' Sara tried to sound convincing.

'Goodbye, your majesties!' Larris bowed and led the villagers back.

'All set?' Welna asked. 'Think so,' said Sara doubtfully as they headed towards the cave.

15

'Oh my God!' cried Crystal as they entered the cave.

'Whoa!' shouted Sara.

Jasmine gave a contented bark as if to say '*Cool! This is so my style!*'

All of them stared. The inside of the cave was the opposite of what it looked like from the outside. It had a wooden floor that was richly carpeted. Velvet wallpaper lined the uneven cave walls. Plush white seats were placed around the room and crystal chandeliers decorated the ceiling. A wooden staircase led down to a lower floor. The same staircase continued upwards to a floor with the bedrooms. Sara took a deep breath; the cave smelt of concentrated lavender and white musk.

'Let's finish this fast and get out of here!' Welna said.

'The cave is so pretty. Can't we stay right here?' asked Crystal dreamily.

Sara stared at her. 'Have you lost it?' she hissed. 'Come

on!' She pulled her towards the staircase that led downstairs.

They looked around nervously half expecting to see someone.

But no one was around. A bead of sweat snaked its way down Sara's spine making her shiver.

As they climbed down the staircase, Sara noticed, with an increasing sense of discomfort, that there were no traces of guards or of the creature himself.

Finally they came to the end of the stairs which opened out into a long corridor lined with life-sized portraits. The walls were scarlet. Fluorescent lights glittered over every portrait. The floor was exquisite oak wood. Looking down the corridor gave Sara a headache. Jasmine too whimpered at the thought of going in there. She blinked her eyes a few times, held her forehead between her thumb and index finger and pressed it hard to get rid of the headache. They started walking down the corridor. Every other second, one of them would look over her shoulder, reasonably sure that someone would be there waiting, with a sword in hand.

Welna shivered as she looked at the various portraits. They were vividly coloured images depicting various kinds of torture. There were pictures of men ripping the guts out of live animals, of people mutilating enemies in terrible ways and images of slaves screaming in agony as their masters skinned them alive, of noblemen holding the severed heads of animals and people. Blood-stained bodies and cold-blooded murder—all of it was there.

'Who is this creature who enjoys torture so much?' Welna wondered as she saw her nieces glance fearfully at the pictures.

They were almost at the end of the corridor now, only two

portraits remained in front of them. Up front, the corridor turned right.

Suddenly, Welna stopped dead in her tracks. Sara and Crystal almost ran into her. Jasmine, walking next to Welna, also stopped and turned in confusion.

They saw that she was staring at the last two portraits. One was of a woman of icy beauty, kneeling down in the snow and petting a white, Arctic wolf. She was dressed entirely in white in a mink coat and a white belt with a snowflake buckle wound around her waist. Her hard blue eyes stared at them, haughty and challenging. Long silvery hair spilled onto her milky bluish-white skin, streaked with loud bubblegum pink highlights. Altogether, the portrait looked very familiar.

The portrait next to it was of a brutal looking man in old-fashioned clothing with fat ugly lips and skin that sagged. His head had an untidy mop of straw-coloured hair and a large, handlebar moustache ran above his upper lip. His scowling eyes were pale grey with shaggy eyebrows that almost hid their gaze. His arms bulged under his heavy coat, underlining the layers of muscle underneath.

'Is that—' Sara began.

'I think that's—' Crystal started. Both of them stood staring at the first portrait.

'Skadi,' Welna said. 'I can't believe I forgot this!'

She pointed to the second picture. 'This is Skadi's father's home. His name is Thjazi,' she explained. 'He is a mountain giant who kidnapped Idunn in the ancient myths. The gods murdered him.'

'So what does this mean?' asked Sara. 'So Thjazi like all other mythical creatures has come back alive? That's it, isn't it?'

'It means,' Welna warned. 'That we have to get out of here fast and avoid a fight with him. Weapons out, ladies.' Her own sword materialized in her hands as the girls turned their bracelets into their weapons.

Sara whistled Jasmine to heel as Crystal nocked an arrow on her bow.

'I'm going ahead,' Sara and Jasmine ran ahead with Welna and Crystal close behind them. They turned with the path and stopped.

'There is a prison cell over there,' Sara said over her shoulder to Welna and Crystal.

She could barely make out the weak glow of an oil lamp coming from far down the corridor. Its light was just enough to illuminate the iron bars of a prison.

Just as Sara and Jasmine were about to run into the corridor, Crystal lost her grip on her arrow and shot it through the air accidentally.

A thousand things happened at once. Lasers criss-crossed the air for a few feet in front of them. Panels opened in the walls from which spears and spurts of acid shot out. A hole appeared in front of them as the floor caved in and at the end of the corridor, an invisible trap door opened and released various kinds of scorpions and spiders.

'Oh—my—god!' Sara gasped, staring cross-eyed at a laser beam just inches away from her nose.

Crystal and Welna stared at the traps set before them, glad that Sara had not ran ahead. 'Sometimes mistakes are for the good', said Crystal feebly.

'How are we supposed to navigate this?' she added after a pause as Jasmine backed away fearfully.

'"So…who's up for some gymnastics?' Welna asked with a wan smile on her pale face.

~

'Ohh….whoa…help!' Crystal shouted as she did a backflip and landed right next to a laser beam, tottering precariously. Jasmine leaned against Crystal, providing her with the support that she needed to stay standing.

'Thanks—' Crystal forced Jasmine's tail back down to prevent it from hitting another beam.

And so they danced their way in and out of the laser beams and finally stepped on to clear territory. Just ahead of them were the opened panels from which spears jutted out and squirts of acid were being released.

'Now what?' asked Sara.

'Why is it that I'm the one who has to do all the thinking?' asked Welna.

'Shields,' said Crystal. 'That's what we need! They'll protect us.'

'Brilliant!' Sara said and unclasped her bracelet. She concentrated and soon enough, she felt her arm grow heavy and opened her eyes to see that she was holding a heavy metal shield. Crystal held a similar one and in Welna's hands was a white shield.

'Jasmine, heel! And stay beside me at all times even though you might be too short to get hit by the arrows,' Crystal ordered.

'Come closer,' said Welna as she pulled both Sara and Crystal closer to her. Their arms were now touching one another's. Sara was to the left of Welna and Crystal to the right. 'Hold your shields in a way that they cover us from all sides,' said Welna. Sara held her shield towards her left, Crystal to the right. Welna held her shield above her head, forming a protective layer around them. Then they made a mad dash to the other end intensely aware of the acid that squirted through holes in the side walls and the sharp weaponry that was being thrown at them.

Just a few feet left…only a couple of steps more…but Crystal was running too fast.

'Crystal, slow down!' Welna warned. They had passed the panels and up ahead was the empty pit.

Sara stopped and bent over, a burning stitch at her waist. But Crystal didn't, or couldn't, stop. Sara saw the panic in her eyes as Crystal skidded past her and she knew at once that she had lost control. Crystal tried to stop at the edge of the pit but lost balance and promptly fell in. The protection that Crystal's shield offered on the right side was gone. They were exposed. Thankfully they were past the area Sara looked on horrified as Crystal disappeared into the pit. What it held inside, no one knew. Luckily, Crystal didn't let go of her shield, which was too large to fall into the pit with her. It stuck at the mouth of the pit, leaving Crystal precariously hanging from it.

As she looked down, Crystal realized to her horror that the bottom of the pit had spears sticking out of it that would rip her body to shreds if she fell.

'Why is it that you always fall down a pit?' asked Sara in exasperation as she hoisted Crystal up.

'You wanna trade places?' Crystal shot back.

They carefully circumvented the pit and stopped short.

Just ahead of them was the horde of scorpions and spiders.

'Oh my god! Do we *have* to go through that?' asked Crystal, worriedly.

'Music,' Welna murmured. 'This is easy.'

'Are you kidding? Maybe once in a while we get lucky,' Sara said.

Welna produced a tiny device from which came soft, sleepy music that gradually filled the room.

The scorpions and spiders scuttled around for a minute and then fell silent.

Shuddering, the girls carefully picked their way through them, careful not to wake them up.

As they stepped over the last scorpion, a wave seemed to run through the blanket of scorpions and spiders as the first few of them shook themselves awake. Jasmine looked at them curiously and gnashed her teeth experimentally.

'No! Jasmine! You are *not* going to eat them!' Sara said, horrified, motioning for Jasmine to walk ahead.

As soon as they crossed the hurdles and stepped ahead, the wooden floor gave way to rocky earth and the painted walls turned into jagged rock.

Just ahead, in a tiny pool of light, was a cell with iron bars.

'Come on! Let's just go and get Idunn. I don't want to stay here for longer than necessary,' Crystal said hurrying forward.

'Wait!' Sara caught Crystal's wrist. 'Welna's right. Isn't this a bit too easy? I mean yes, there were traps but none of them took us more than a minute to find a solution for!'

'Listen, maybe it *is* a bit too easy. Maybe that's a problem, maybe it's not. That's why I want to get out of this place fast,' Crystal said. Sara let go of Crystal's wrist and after exchanging a worried glance with Welna, she ran behind her.

The door to the cell was locked.

Welna tried every spell that she could think of, but nothing opened the door. They could see nothing inside, not even the source of the mysterious pool of light. Disheartened, Jasmine plonked himself down on the cold floor and stared up at them dolefully.

'Maybe...maybe where a magical solution doesn't work, a human solution will!' said Crystal suddenly.

She reached behind Welna and in a swift stroke pulled out the tiny jewelled hairpin that held Welna's hair in place.

As Welna's hair tumbled down, Crystal inserted the hairpin inside the keyhole and jiggled it around for a while. Then, with a satisfying click, the cell door swung open inwards on its hinges.

'Uh...' Welna started to say as Sara's heart thudded with excitement.

Lightly, treading cautiously, the three stepped over the threshold of the prison—and stepped into a completely new world.

The girls staggered as their vision went fizzy, like static on the T.V. Then everything came back to them in high quality like someone had just tuned in.

They were in a different place. This wasn't a dingy prison cell—it was an extremely chic suite.

Sara's first thought on seeing it was, 'Wow! I could go to prison just for this!' and immediately felt embarrassed.

The hall was humongous with vibrant splashes of colour. Comfy armchairs and bean bags lay scattered on a huge fuchsia rug. A cream sofa set with two cushiony chairs was set in the centre of the room around a low, polished wooden table set with an assortment of foods. A winding marble staircase led to the floor above. State-of-the-art stereos, speakers and sound equipment adorned various parts of the room along with a stately fountain beside the staircase.

Books, paintings, CDs, instruments and various tools hung on the walls, while lava lamps were positioned strategically.

The door of an adjoining room was ajar and the girls could just about see a four poster bed hung with gold drapes and a dresser with an ornate mirror.

'Classy,' Crystal said with an admiring nod. 'And to think it looked like a godforsaken cell from outside!'

'Woof! Woof!' Jasmine barked joyfully pleased to see a sophisticated, earth-like place.

'So...I have visitors,' said a disembodied voice suddenly.

The girls and Welna turned around in alarm.

Coming down the stairs was an elegant woman. She was at least six feet tall with a slim figure and long legs. Her bright, blue-green eyes were almost completely hidden under her choppy, windswept, copper hair that was cut short with bangs. A purple spaghetti top and a pair of denim shorts showed off her perfectly tanned skin and round shoulders. Her bare feet treaded softly on the wooden stairs and she wore a smile on her glowing face.

'Uh...um...actually...Sara?' Crystal stuttered. She didn't know why the woman was so awe inspiring, but there was something in her face the way she walked, the way she talked, that was captivating.

'Idunn?' asked Sara.

'Ah...you know my name!' said Idunn with a smile.

'Idunn, I'm Welna, the wind princess of Catriona,' Welna said formally and Idunn nodded.

'We have come to rescue you out of your prison. Come on, let's get going before Thjazi comes!' Crystal said in a rush, remembering her purpose.

'Prison? Rescue me? Why would I want that?' Idunn asked, her eyes widening in surprise.

'Wha—what do you mean?' Sara asked, confused.

'Why would I want to get out of here? I have everything, all the luxuries in life, including my own house and Thjazi has never ill-treated me!' Idunn replied.

'But...in the myths...Thjazi kidnapped you! He's working for Merissa!' Welna reasoned. 'He'll want to give those apples to Merissa to make her young again!'

'Why should I be bothered?' Idunn asked studying her perfect nails intently.

'Well, with a deranged god about to bring about an improvised Ragnarok, and the fact that our mothers are in prison and the Norse gods who will undoubtedly begin to age without your apples, you *should* be bothered,' said Sara.

Idunn's eyes flashed with anger and she stared at Sara—a gesture obviously meant to intimidate—but Sara stared right back.

Jasmine stepped forward and bared her teeth. She didn't like anyone getting too pushy with Sara.

'If you're trying to persuade me to leave my lavish *prison*, then your attitude is really not helping!' Idunn said, running a lazy hand through her hair.

'Sara,' Welna warned.

'Why would you want to stay trapped in here for all

eternity and get killed by Loki? We give you a chance of freedom and you just hand it back? No one in their right mind would do that!' Sara said, taking a deep breath. 'If you don't come with us, we don't get the Aquamarine gem. If we don't get the gem then we can't make the Moon Wand. And if we don't make the Moon Wand, the world is going to end!'

'You are making the Moon Wand?' Idunn asked, suddenly paying attention. 'Have the problems of the world become so serious? But why *you*? Did Odin force you to do this? He's always doing things like this, forc—' Idunn ranted on.

'Loki,' Crystal said firmly, 'killed our fathers. And Merissa has locked up our mothers in a musty cellar prison—nothing as posh as yours!'

'Then this is serious! We need to get out of here now!' Idunn said abruptly. Sara nodded, a little surprised.

'No turning into a nut then?' asked Crystal.

'Nut? Are you serious! No way! Last time was *very* uncomfortable!' Idunn retorted .

'Come on then!'

Together they stepped out of the prison-suite into the red corridor and came face-to-face with Thjazi.

~

He looked exactly like his portrait: ugly, brutish and scowling.

Jasmine growled menacingly at him and snapped her teeth but he didn't even spare her a look. In a moment, Sara had her sword in her hand but Thjazi was too quick for her. He caught her by the neck, making strange growling noises in his throat. Sara felt her feet leave the ground as he raised her up, all the while tightening his grip on her throat.

White spots floated in front her eyes. She struggled to breathe and a vein bulged in her throbbing head. Then just as suddenly, she felt a sharp pain in her back as she fell to floor with an unceremonious thud.

Crystal had jabbed at Thjazi with her own sword. Sara found her voice and shouted, '*Run*! Let's get outta here!'

They sprinted through the red corridor as fast as they could, the portraits all a blurry streak as they raced past.

'Go, go, go!' Idunn urged as she dashed past them and started climbing the stairs. A streak of white that was Jasmine leapt after Idunn.

'Idunn! You dare betray me?' Thjazi bellowed as he chased after them.

He was gaining on them. Sara knew she wouldn't be able to make it but she ran on.

Idunn had made it to the top. Crystal was next, followed by Welna.

Thjazi roared again.

A string of words in an unknown language poured out of Thjazi's mouth and suddenly, Crystal slipped on the stairs and fell straight back, crashing into Welna who in turn, crashed into Sara.

They landed in a heap at the foot of the stairs

Sara opened her eyes and rubbed her head. A shadow fell on them as Thjazi's huge form towered over them.

'Now I shall send your heads to Merissa as well, along with Idunn's golden apples!' Thjazi smiled, showing his rotting teeth 'No! My apples are mine alone. And I shall give them only to those I choose,' Idunn said from the top of the stairs. 'Now face my wrath!'

A golden beam of light shot from her outstretched palm and raced towards Thjazi. But he deflected it with a lazy flick of his hand.

'*I* kidnapped you Idunn! I know all your tricks! Surrender and I might not harm you!' Thjazi said imperiously as Sara, Crystal and Welna scrambled to their feet, weapons in their hands.

Idunn, meanwhile, was half-kneeling, with her hands on her forehead, pressing hard to relieve herself of the pain that had suddenly taken over. Jasmine was nudging her with her nose.

'Come on! He's sapping my magic! I will be powerless until I get my apples back,' Idunn shouted.

The girls needed no more encouragement. They turned and raced up the stairs and into the drawing room.

But as they were about to move further, gigantic, jagged rocks appeared in front of them even as Thjazi came sprinting up the stairs.

'Crystal, destroy the rocks! Welna and I will keep Thjazi distracted!' Sara screamed. 'And Jasmine, cover Crystal.' Jasmine obediently leapt into position in front of Crystal.

'You will be no match for Thjazi,' Idunn warned ominously.

'You have a better plan?' challenged Sara. She was utterly bugged now. Why did everything they they did turn out to be dangerous? She had never asked for adventure!

Sara stepped forward to meet Thjazi. Thjazi's sword materialized in his hand and the two weapons clashed with a loud clang.

The next few minutes were a blur in Sara's memory. She only remembered fighting with everything she had. Thjazi and Sara wove in and out of reach of each other's swords in a kind of crude dance as they slashed and parried.

Meanwhile Crystal concentrated hard on the rocks. She commanded them to break, to crumble into fine dust.

'Break, you stupid piece of rock!' she thought, but her thoughts wandered.'Oh, I hope Sara is okay...I wonder how Welna is doing...' She opened her eyes and there the rocks were, as large as life, showing no signs of crumbling. Her magic had not worked.

'Crystal! You *have* to concentrate,' Idunn lectured.

Crystal sighed and tried again. Welna and Sara were having a tough time keeping Thjazi occupied. When it came to sword fighting, Thajzi was surprisingly agile, despite his bulky form.They were hard pressed to keep him at bay. They had to have perfect timing, strategy and perfect moves. Thjazi just needed that one opening, that one single mistake from either of them to have them cornered.

In a particularly difficult manoeuvre, Thjazi did something completely unexpected. He thrust his sword at Welna which she easily parried but instead of disengaging, he forced her sword into a circular move and she unexpectedly dropped her sword. Sara's sword too went skittering across the floor and he held Welna's and his own sword both to Sara's and Welna's throats.

Crystal, unaware of all of this, was still deep in concentration. She imagined herself tapping into the energy source that was her magic and immersed herself in it. Then she channeled her energy onto the rocks to the point of bursting and beyond. And then suddenly with a sonic boom, the rocks shattered.

'Yes! I did I—,' Crystal turned to see Sara and Welna at sword point, Jasmine growling and Idunn standing very still and looking like she was about to be sick.

Crystal put her hands behind her back casually.

'Leave them, Thjazi!' she said softly. She felt her hands grow heavier as her bow expanded in her hands from her bracelet.

'Or what?' Thjazi mocked.

Her quiver materialized in front of her and she swiftly shot two arrows: one at each sword. Thjazi was taken by surprise. One of his swords fell to the floor while the other was thrown off balance.

'Run!' Crystal shouted and ran towards the door.

Sara, Idunn and Jasmine started to sprint but Welna stayed a split second more to summon Sara's and Welna's swords back to her. And that split second almost cost her, her life.

Recovering from his surprise, Thjazi focused on the only living creature nearest to him: Welna.

With a roar of anger, he threw his long sword right at her.

For a moment Welna stood rooted to the spot as the sword hurtled closer and closer towards her and would have certainly slit her throat. It was too late to move out of the way. Was it the end of Welna? Suddenly, out of the blue she did something that none of them expected.

She struck her neck, breaking a tiny, glistening orb from her necklace and screamed a name—

'SKADI!'

16

There was a flash of light and in front of Welna stood a beautiful woman with white blond hair and cold blue eyes.

'Hello, Father,' she said casually putting out her hand to catch the sword that would have impaled Welna. 'Nice to meet you again,' she lazily examined the weapon.

'Skadi! Get away from her! I need to deal with them!' Thjazi growled.

'Not before you deal with me, Father,' Skadi looked up, her eyes flashing. 'Go, girls. My father and I have some unfinished business. And Idunn…it's been a long time since I last met you. As beautiful as ever I see.'

'Skadi…' Sara whispered suddenly, full of reverence for the goddess.

'*Go!*' Skadi ordered Sara. Her voice left no room for argument.

The girls turned and ran half-heartedly out of the room.

'Father…why not be on my side?' they heard Skadi reason.

There was a loud bang and they heard Skadi scream.

'So be it, Father! If you want to fight, here I am!' they heard Skadi shout and suddenly, the whole house started shaking.

'Not good. Not good at all! Too much magical energy,' Welna muttered. 'We need to find the apples fast.'

'Where do you think they'll be?' asked Sara.

'Where do you think apples are kept?' Idunn asked nonchalantly.

'The kitchen!' Welna gasped. Jasmine bounded ahead with a bark of joy as the girls followed.

~

The apples were not there. They searched everywhere but couldn't find them.

The house was shaking and pieces of the roof were beginning to cave in. Time was running out. The roof of the adjoining hall collapsed with a crash. The kitchen was next, the roof had already begun to collapse. The far wall of the kitchen caved with a thud.

'Hurry up!' said Sara panicking. A huge chunk of the roof fell next to Crystal's foot.

'Watch out!' screamed Sara, as a huge slab above the refrigerator began to collapse. Welna ducked into a niche behind the refrigerator. The slab crashed violently into the refrigerator and smashed it to pieces.

'Welna!' screamed Sara. She was worried as she hadn't known that Welna had ducked into the niche.

When the dust settled, Welna emerged from the niche. Sara and Crystal heaved sighs of relief.

'Let's get out of here', said Crystal, 'The apples are not here.'

'They *have* to be here!' Idunn shouted as she dropped to the floor to avoid the debris falling on her.

'Let's go!' said Sara urgently.

'Woof woof!' They were about to leave the kitchen when Jasmine's bark stopped them. They turned. Jasmine stood facing the niche where Welna had taken shelter against the falling slab. Sara rushed back to pick Jasmine up.

As she bent down, she froze. Behind the ruined refrigerator, hidden beneath the rubble, was the basket of golden apples. Her eyes grew round and wide and she screamed out to Welna and Crystal.

'They're here! Welna, they were right behind you in the niche,' she called out. Welna and Crystal rushed back, grinning. All of them had wide grins on their faces as Welna grabbed the baskets full of golden apples. Even in this situation, Sara couldn't help but notice how beautiful they were, shining gold and lustrous. As they ran towards the living room, the entire kitchen started to collapse inwards. They ran towards the door leading out of the cave as the living room started imploding. Paintings were wrenched from the walls and thrown on the ground. Drapes collapsed, columns were uprooted and chandeliers dropped to the floor. They made a dash for the entrance and when they finally reached the door they gasped. They could still hear Skadi and Thjazi fighting.

The sky was tinged pink. 'No way! We couldn't have been down there for a whole day! It's dawn now!' Sara said in disbelief. Jasmine, who was already out of the door barked in anxiety. But they hardly had time to admire the dawn because just as they stepped out, the whole cave gave in. A falling rock hit Crystal's feet and she screamed in pain. Sara and Welna were already out by then. Soon enough, the entire entrance collapsed into a pile of rubble.

'Crystal!' Sara screamed. Crystal hadn't made it out!

Sara screamed and fought to go back to get Crystal, but it was too dangerous and Welna held her back with tears in her eyes. She sat down heavily on a tree stump and started weeping while Welna stood there watching. Idunn too looked at Sara sympathetically. Finally Sara stopped weeping and stared blankly ahead. Jasmine went to the edge of the hill and howled mournfully. Jasmine licked Sara's hand in a vain attempt to cheer her up.

Then someone tapped Sara's shoulder.

'Welna, I just want to be alone,' Sara whispered. Someone tapped her again.

Sara whirled around intending to tell Welna to leave her alone for a little while. 'Welna, I just asked you to leave...' The moment she turned she started screaming.

In front of her stood a very familiar person covered in dust. She coughed.

'Crystal!' Sara hugged her and started weeping all over again. Welna laughed. Jasmine went mad, jumping and pawing Crystal till she finally bent down and hugged her. Even Idunn managed a smile though she had a distant look in her eyes.

'What happened? Why are you all so upset?' Crystal asked confused.

'We thought we had lost you!' Welna said.

Ya I *would* have been under that pile of rubble had I not had these amazing brains of mine!' Crystal said airily, tapping her head. 'Relax guys! God! Trust me; you are not getting rid of me so soon!'

'How did you escape?' Sara asked, letting go of Crystal.

'I'll show you.'

She led them to what had once been the entrance to the cave.

There, propped against a huge stone was a silver gleaming sword. Crystal had turned her bracelet into a sword at the last minute and had used it to prop up the huge stone so that the entrance of the cave wasn't completely blocked. Now she walked up to the entrance and snapped her hands. The sword turned back into a bracelet and she caught it lightly before the stone fell and closed off the mouth of the cave forever.

'Crystal, you're limping!' Welna said suddenly noticing Crystal's leg.

'A rock fell on my leg.'

'Come here,' Welna instructed her to sit down. She then took her leg in her hand. She nodded to Sara who began to talk to Crystal about their mothers. As soon as Crystal was distracted, Welna gave the leg a sharp twist. 'Ow!' Crystal howled. 'What are you trying to do?'

'That trick always works!' Idunn said as she watched Crystal standing up gingerly. It was the first time she had spoken since they got out of the cave.

Jasmine must have found the sight really comical for she cocked her head to one side and peeled her lips back in a doggie smile. Sara laughed.

'Wait a second!' said Crystal, 'The pain's gone! What did you do?' She hugged Welna.

'Nothing, I just twisted it the other way', smiled Welna.

'Now let's get going,' said Sara, suddenly cheerful. 'Let's go get the gem!'

They all laughed happily. The hike down to the village was a pleasant one; they were exhausted but happy. Jasmine trotted along happily, occasionally drifting away to tease a rabbit or two.

~

The old woman who Sara had helped spotted them first. She raised an alarm and by the time they entered the tiny village, there was quite a crowd to meet them. They all stared in wonder as they saw the goddess towering above them. 'You came back!' Larris shouted and did a cartwheel. The girls clapped in approval.

After all the explanations, the golden apples were handed to the villagers. Finally they sat down to a scrumptious breakfast. Jasmine was greeted with much joy the Cilicians who were once scared of her had grown quite fond of her. She enjoyed the attention and even gave the officers a ride.

They introduced the Cilicians to Idunn. Idunn, having finally got back her apples, was positively glowing.

'I need to go back to Asgard,' said the goddess. She turned on the spot and was surrounded by a golden aura. When she faced Sara and Crystal again, they gasped. Idunn had changed into her goddess form. Her choppy copper hair was now long and luscious, with soft curls that brushed her cheeks. She wore an emerald green gown laced with tiny pearls that matched her blue-green eyes. Her face was glowing and a tint of pink gloss was visible on her lips. Dark kohl circled her eyes while a dusting of bronze eye shadow accentuated her whole face. She snapped her fingers and another basket of golden apples appeared in her hand.

One by one, the Cilicians knelt down before her as did Sara, Crystal and Welna.

'Cilicians, I am proud of your hard work, skills and energy. I gift you my golden apples and you may use them as you deem fit,' Idunn's voice was warm and melodious. She then turned to the girls.

'Girls, I bless you with luck and thank you for rescuing me from my prison, lovely as it was.' Idunn smiled at the girls and they grinned. 'Loki shall never succeed with you here to stop him!'

'Farewell. I shall make known to the gods and goddesses of Norse, those who are still uncorrupted by Loki, that there are some truly wonderful people in this kingdom.' Idunn vanished in a puff of golden vapour.

'What about Skadi?' Sara asked suddenly.

As if on cue, the ruins of Thjazi's cave exploded in fire in the distance. The girls sat up straight and looked on in horror.

'Skadi has gone to Hel, the Norse place of death, along with her father. I doubt whether her father will rise again but I know that Skadi will come back. And this time she won't be bound to Loki. But it will take time.' Welna said soberly.

The Cilicians, however, seemed unconcerned with the exploding cave and continued with their merrymaking. Finally, when they were done with the festivities, Welna asked Larris, 'Now can we have the gem?'

At this Larris stammered, 'Um...a-a-actually y-you have to do one more t-t-thing,'

'What?' Crystal yelled in frustration. '*More* things?'

'What do we have to do?' demanded Sara.

'You have to choose the right gem from the Lake of

Lotuses,' Larris said sheepishly.

'Take us there! Now!' Welna ordered.

'This is ridiculous. Why didn't you tell us this earlier?"

Without waiting to answer her query, Larris ran to get the other officers and villagers and all of them led the girls to the far end of the village to a lake, the prettiest that Sara and Crystal had ever seen. But prettier than the lake were the ten lotuses that floated in its clear blue water. The lotuses were not pink or white, but a pale aquamarine and in the centre of each was a big, blue, beautiful aquamarine stone.

'This is the Lake of Lotuses,' said Larris. 'You get only one chance to choose the right gem.'

'But all of these are gems!' Crystal protested.

'All of them are gems, but only one belongs to the Moon Wand,' Larris explained. 'Now choose!'

'Woof!' Jasmine barked, as if to say, 'Hey, that's not fair!'

Neither girl spoke. Sara chewed her lips in frustration.

'That one! It glitters the most! It has to be that one,' Crystal cried suddenly. 'Larris! It's that one!'

'Which one, your highness?' Larris asked, confused.

Sara was trying to concentrate. She couldn't make up her mind.

'There, that one! I think the fifth, no sixth, one!' Crystal said.

'Ah, I see! Is that your final choice?' Larris asked.

'Of course it's my final choice!' Crystal said, impatiently.

'Connor! Bring us the lotus! Let us examine it!' Larris said.

'No, wait!' cried Sara suddenly. 'That's not the right one! All that glitters is not gold, Crystal. The last one, the tenth one, is the right one!'

'No!' cried Crystal. 'Why do you think it's that one?'

'Because Mum told me in my dreams! The one with their reflections etched in them is the real gem!' Sara said and narrated the dream to all of them. 'Look!' And sure enough, the reflections of two female figures glinted in the rising sun.

'Choose one, ladies!' said Larris, amused.

'The tenth!' said Sara and Crystal together.

Larris got the lotus and examined it. His face lit up as he handed the gem to the girls. 'It's the right one!' he shouted and the village erupted in applause.

Sara looked carefully at the smooth round gem in her hands, etched with her mother's and aunt's reflections. It was the colour of moonlight.

'Where are we going to keep this? We need to keep this in a safe place,' she said.

'You'll find out soon enough,' said Welna.

Hardly had she said this, when the stone started to grow hot in Sara's hand. She opened up her hand, the stone was lying in the centre of her palm. It was becoming too hot for her to bear. Suddenly, as if to relieve her, the stone floated up. Then the most astonishing thing happened—it split into two perfect circles, each with an image of a queen.

The stones then flew towards the two girls, approaching them like tiny ball of fire. For an instant the two girls were scared. Welna held Sara's and Crystal's hands tightly, as if to say, *Don't worry, I am here.*

The two stones advanced towards the girls and flew at their necks. The girls closed their eyes, afraid. Then they heard a tiny click. When they opened their eyes, they were astonished. The two stones had snapped themselves safely into one of the empty holes in each of their necklaces! The half stone with Anastasia's reflection had snapped itself into Sara's while the one with Olivia's reflection had snapped itself into Crystal's. Welna nodded approvingly. This was how it was supposed to be.

~

That night, as Welna sharpened her wind sword and Sara and Crystal lay in their grassy makeshift bed, Sara thought happily about how they had got their first gem working together, as a team. She wondered what she would have done without Welna and Crystal. As she settled down to sleep, she touched her necklace out of habit and the smooth stone embedded inside it felt cold against her skin. Jasmine was snoring contentedly between Crystal and Sara. She had had quite a day.

Suddenly Sara sat up, a mischievous smile lighting up her face. They were planning to stay on in Cilicia for another day. Now that they had found the Aquamarine gem, they had a little time to have fun and Sara knew exactly what she was going to do...

She glanced at Crystal who was snoring. Perfect. She imagined Crystal's face painted like a clown with an unusually large red nose. In moments Crystal's face was painted. Sara materialized a spray of shaving cream in her hand and very gently sprayed it over Crystal's hand. She then whispered in Crystal's ear, 'Crystal, there is a huge mosquito on your nose.' Instinctively Crystal slapped her hand on her nose. The shaving cream landed on her nose with a huge wet splat! Crystal sat up and screamed and in the process swallowed some of it too!

'What—is—on—my—face?' Crystal spluttered.

'Shaving cream!' Sara replied calmly.

Welna joined in. 'Crystal! I didn't know you had a beard! Especially one on your nose that you had to use shaving cream to take it off!' she said with a perfectly straight face. She snapped her finger and a mirror appeared in front of Crystal. She grasped it and screamed even louder! It made the villagers far away stir in their sleep.

'Who did this?' Crystal asked. Sara's expression gave her away. Crystal put her hands on her hips which made her look even funnier as her face was painted like a clown with a red nose sticking out.

'Uh-huh sis! Nice prank, huh? Now how about some revenge? Maybe I could turn you into a grasshopper. No, a toad, how about that?'

'Oh no! You wouldn't!' Sara said, getting up alarmed.

'Oh yeah? Try me!' Crystal retorted, jumping up to catch Sara.

Any Cilician who saw the two girls laughing and running around under the clear night sky, with a very confused looking dog barking her head off, would wonder what was wrong. The girls were beautiful though one of them looked like she had got a huge boil on her nose which had been splattered with shaving cream. A young lady stood to one side laughing as the girls ran around.

But no one would have ever guessed that they were the princesses, Crystal and Sara, heirs of Catriona, and the young lady beside them was their aunt, Princess Welna, the wind goddess! And that all four of them were celebrating the end of their first adventure.

The full moon climbed higher into the dark, velvet blanket

of the sky and cast its glow onto the valley below as if smiling affectionately. The quest for the Aquamarine gem was over and all the girls needed now was a good night's sleep before they headed off to find the other three gems in their quest to defeat Merissa.

Acknowledgements

'Life is not about the destination, it's about the journey,' Ralph Waldo Emerson had once said. But the true meaning of these words is becoming clear to me only now. Writing this book has been one of the most exciting things I have attempted in my life. It has occupied my thoughts ever since I wrote the first words. The elation that I felt on completing the manuscript was nothing compared to the joy I felt while writing it. Hours of dreaming about various descriptions, contemplating alternate scenarios at every stage, worrying about grammatical errors, and knowing I had this to get back to once I was home from school made me look forward to each day of the journey.

However, there were many others who made it possible for me to get this book to the stage it is in now.

My constant sources of inspiration were the works of Rick Riordan and J.K. Rowling. Reading their books made me want to write too. And I definitely couldn't have done so without my parents' support. Thank you Mom, for putting up with me while I stayed up late working on the manuscript; and Dad, for being a constant source of encouragement and inspiration. I am indebted to my friends, Neeti, Meghna and and especially Varun and Kirtana—who were amongst the first to read my manuscript—for their unending enthusiasm and valuable feedback.

I consider myself lucky to have had the opportunity to have worked alongside Sudeshna Shome Ghosh, who edited *Heirs of Catriona*. She single-handedly made a huge difference to the book and to me as an author. Thanks for everything, Sudeshna.

And finally to my grandparents in Chennai and Delhi, thank you for being constantly willing to listen to my stories—which were sometimes just pointless ramblings—and goading me on to complete this novel, the first of many more to come.

About the Author

One of the country's youngest published authors, Anusha Subramanian was twelve when she wrote *Heirs of Catriona* and sixteen when she wrote her second book, *Never Gone*. After graduating from a leading International School in Mumbai, she completed her undergraduate education at University of California, Berkeley, graduating with a major in Molecular and Cellular Biology (Genetics) and a minor in Data Science. During her time there, she wrote for *The Daily Californian* as well as the *Berkeley Scientific Journal*, both renowned collegiate reporting communities. Her interests and hobbies stretch across interdisciplinary fields including but not limited to computational biology, psychology, data science, creative writing, reading, art and community service. Currently she's conducting immunology research at a leading institution in California. You can connect with her on Twitter @Anusha0712.

30 Years *of*
HarperCollins *Publishers* India

At HarperCollins, we believe in telling the best stories and finding the widest possible readership for our books in every format possible. We started publishing 30 years ago; a great deal has changed since then, but what has remained constant is the passion with which our authors write their books, the love with which readers receive them, and the sheer joy and excitement that we as publishers feel in being a part of the publishing process.

Over the years, we've had the pleasure of publishing some of the finest writing from the subcontinent and around the world, and some of the biggest bestsellers in India's publishing history. Our books and authors have won a phenomenal range of awards, and we ourselves have been named Publisher of the Year the greatest number of times. But nothing has meant more to us than the fact that millions of people have read the books we published, and somewhere, a book of ours might have made a difference.

As we step into our fourth decade, we go back to that one word – a word which has been a driving force for us all these years.

Read.